Sam Mouse

Craig Turner

Sam Mouse

ISBN-13: 978-0-9944596-0-2
Published by Paxel Publishing
https://www.paxel.com.au
PO Box 9172, Axedale, Vic, Australia 3551

Paxel Publishing

To my beautiful wife and family,

You let me give life to Sam,

In giving life to Sam, you gave life to a host of dreams.

Thank you for your support, tolerance and putting up with me trying (unsuccessfully) to get out of bed quietly at 5am

I love you all.

This edition, my first print book, is especially dedicated to my son, Tommy on his first birthday.

Happy Birthday Tommy!

Credits

Cover design by: D&J Designs

Editing by: Bubble Cow

Proofreading: Campbell & Ava

Table of Contents

Chapter One - A Letter Arrives

Sam was rather annoyed as he tore open the letter, making a slight muttering sound, his whiskers twitching in annoyance. "Dear me, this is no good, no good at all," he said. The rather formal looking letter, printed on a lovely cream parchment, was from the Committee for the Protection of Mice (and affiliated rodents), Sub Branch 27.

Sam would be the first to acknowledge that from time-to-time the committee had done some fine work. Most fine. Indeed, if it were not for the committee, Sam himself might not be alive today. But it doesn't take a wise mouse to know that a letter from the committee wasn't something that happened every day.

"Oh dear," he said as he read. "Oh dear. They've passed a resolution."

Sam wasn't the wisest of mice, nor perhaps the most politically astute, but he certainly knew, like we all do, that once committees get it into their heads to do things such as pass resolutions, why who knows what will happen next?

In the floweriest of prose, with much 'thereforing' and not a little 'henceforthing', and just a smidgen of 'wherefore', the letter proclaimed that the Committee for the Protection of Mice (and affiliated rodents), Sub Branch 27, did declare, on behalf of all Mice (and affiliated rodents) that there was a 'rogue cat', who was killing mice and that this cat must be dealt with, and dealt with in no uncertain terms, so that all mice (and affiliated rodents) could 'henceforth enjoy such pursuits that mice (and affiliated rodents) did choose to undertake, for the further pursuit of happiness, and for the furtherance of all mice etc. etc. etc.'.

Sam came to the section dealing with exactly how the committee intended to deal with the cat. Sam gave a squeak, this time quite clearly shrill as he read that the committee had selected a mouse to deal with the cat. But no ordinary mouse. Indeed, the mouse was to be a noble mouse, a mouse of impeccable breeding, most admirably suited to out smarting such a cat. A cat killer, from a line of cat killers. A champion mouse amongst mice.

Perhaps he could pass on some wisdom to this noble mouse, wisdom that his grandfather had passed on from his battles against the cat, a generation ago. For Sam's grandfather was considered quite an authority when it came to cats. Indeed, Sam was in the middle of writing a book about his grandfather Noah, so he could probably pass on some very good advice. Sam's heart beat quite fast when he thought of his one and only encounter with a cat. He pushed away the thought of those big green eyes staring at him.

With a shrill shriek, Sam dropped the letter and clapped both paws over his eyes. His body shivered, and his tawny fur stood up on end. Uncovering one eye, he bent down and picked up the letter. Holding it by one corner, as if were now dirty, he peered at it again.

He peered, specifically, at the bit that said, quite simply:

> *'The Committee hereby declares Sam Mouse, currently residing at No. 28 Herring Place to be the Champion Mouse. The Committee wishes to be the first to congratulate this most brave mouse on his selection as Champion Mouse and wishes him every success in his endeavors to rid the community of this most vexatious of problems.'*

Sam wondered if there might be another Sam living at an altogether different 28 Herring Place. There was a Sam who lived around the corner, but that was in Cheddar Way, and he preferred to be called Samuel. In fact, he was quite particular on that point. There was also a Herring Drive not far from the laundry, but that was mainly the domain of the rats. Rather slovenly creatures, whom the committee only barely acknowledged to be 'affiliated rodents'. Sam rather thought that the committee would prefer not to nominate a rat as the Champion of Mice. No, it was quite clear that the committee had dear old Sam in mind.

There was a sharp rap at the door. A rather official sounding 'knock'. Sam scurried over to his front door and peered around the corner. With a rather determined push, the door swung open, and a bevy of mice flowed into his parlor.

"Ahh, Sam," proclaimed a rather plump mouse in a tartan waistcoat. "Congratulations my dear fellow. You must be proud. Terribly proud indeed. Mouse Champion eh?" He peered closely at Sam, stopped for a second, then stood back and pumped Sam's paw. "Well my good fellow. How do you plan to do it? Some sort of family secret eh?" The plump fellow gave Sam a rather broad wink.

"Well speak up my good fellow," bellowed a rather grey muzzled old mouse, who held up an ear trumpet at Sam. "What is your plan for this cat?"

Behind the old chap stood a rather large mouse, who Sam thought that rather looked a bit like a rat. Altogether too much like a rat. An impolite mouse might have referred to him as 'rattish', although not Sam, who considered himself quite the refined mouse. Next to the large fellow stood a slim young mouse who looked quite dapper in a fine tweed jacket. Now Sam wasn't one to judge a book by a cover, and he was not known for his hasty decisions, but he immediately decided he didn't like the young fellow. He looked altogether smooth. Yes, thought Sam, this chap is altogether too smooth. What's more, he does look rather young to be on the committee.

The plump mouse, who Sam now noticed had some crumbs of cheese stuck to his waistcoat, continued pumping Sam's paw at an alarming rate. "Names Charles Montagu, old chap, don't bother yourself with all those 'Sir's' or other official titles, Mr Montagu will be just fine." He smiled at Sam. "Now, the committee has a few questions. Nothing complicated, don't want to get in your way. After all, you are the expert."

"Expert? Me? The Expert?" echoed Sam with a gasp.

"Yes, yes, no need to go on about it. We know you're the expert," said the elderly chap with the ear horn. Rather gruffly, Sam thought.

The old mouse sat himself down in Sam's favorite chair. "Young Mice these days. No humility. All ready to tell you how good they are. All show and no substance. Like processed cheese." And at that, he appeared to doze off.

Chapter Two - After The Party

Sam awoke with a sore head. There was a quite distinct pounding in his head that only seemed to get worse as he woke up. His mouth seemed very dry and his fur felt altogether disheveled. He rather fancied that his mouth had been used to clean the floor of a rat's hovel. Not that Sam really believed that rats lived in hovels, nor had particularly dirty floors, but his mouth did feel rather unsavory.

He rolled over to discover that, rather than lying in his soft nest-like bed, he was curled up in his oldest arm chair. He sat up, quite slowly, for somehow sleeping in the arm chair had not been as agreeable to his body as sleeping in his nest was, and it certainly was not helping his poor headache at all. His eyes began to focus on his living room, and he let out a gasp of dismay. Sam was a tidy mouse. Some might say that he was a touch fussy, but Sam liked to think of himself as simply being neat. "Neatness" he would say "is what separates us from the outside animals."

But something rather strange had happened, although his poor eyes had not yet fully focused, Sam noticed with alarm that his lounge room looked messy. Not messy like you might expect after having just got home from a hard day at work, and taken your shoes off without putting them away.

No, Sam's lounge room looked like a rather rough party of rats had used his lounge room for… for, well, for whatever it is that a party of rough rats gets up to in their lounges. Whatever had happened, it had left his lounge room looking very messy indeed. Sam was not only feeling quite sore, but also quite alarmed.

He sat up and with a rather despairing look on his face, he took in the full extent of the desecration of his once comfortable lounge room. Glasses filled with all manner of colored liquid sat on every flat space he could see... except for those flat spaces that were covered by plates and bowls, which in turn were covered in cheeses. Many different cheeses.

Sam spied what appeared to be his favorite Gruyere (cave aged to perfection.) Someone had left a piece of Stilton sitting on it and it had oozed all over the Gruyere. He'd been saving the Gruyere for a special occasion.

Special occasion...it occurred to Sam now, that there WAS a special occasion last night, something about a cat...something about a rather capable mouse who was going to 'take care of the cat'. With a sudden hot flush, Sam's headache got worse as he remembered that HE was the mouse that was going to take care of the cat.

Sam had a sudden memory of telling the party of mice that had gathered at his home how he was going to rid the rodents of the cat. He seemed to recall that his little apartment was quite crowded with other mice at the time, who all seemed to clap and cheer at each of his pronouncements.

Sam moaned and covered his eyes. He remembered standing on his dining table, and proclaiming loudly, and in no uncertain terms, that he would deal with this rather nasty cat and strike a blow for all mice who had suffered at the paws of cats. At that pronouncement, everyone had gone silent for a moment and muttered a quiet 'here here', for they all knew of someone who had suffered. But they had soon slapped Sam on the back and said what a wonderful fellow he was, and the party had gotten louder.

Sam moaned again, and sunk deeper into his lounge chair. Part of his mind wanted to believe that it was all a horrible dream and if he slept for a bit longer it would all go away. But another part of his mind knew, with a very strong sinking feeling, that his memories of the previous night, whilst very hazy, were also accurate.

Sam staggered towards his bedroom, trying hard not to trip over the upturned furniture, and trying even harder not to notice the messy plates and dishes that littered his lovely lounge room. He leaned against the door to his bedroom, thinking how wonderful his nest would be, if he could only manage to walk a few more feet.

Except, there appeared to be another mouse curled up in his nest, wrapped in his favorite blanket. Sam moaned. How could his day get any worse? Who was in his nice, warm, cozy nest? How on earth had Sam agreed to let ANYONE sleep in his nest while he was forced to sleep in his hard reading chair?

There was a faint stirring.

"Hello?" said Sam. "Ahem, ah, hello?" Talking seemed to make his eyes hurt a little bit more.

A corner of the blanket lifted up, and a delicate paw emerged. Sam's eyes opened wide, which, considering how dry they were, caused him some discomfort. A twitching nose appeared. It was rather a delicate nose Sam thought, unlike the nose of any of his friends.

"Ahem, 'er, who is that?"

"Hello Sam," said a voice that sounded as soft as cream cheese. "Thank you for letting me use your nest. I hope you weren't too uncomfortable last night."

"Ahh, no. I was quite comfortable thank you," Sam lied, for he was a polite mouse, "ah, umm, I seem to have... that is I'm not sure… ah ...do I know you?"

"Oh Sam," she looked down at the blanket, and then back up at Sam with a shy smile, "I'm sorry I thought you remembered me… my name is Gypsy."

Sam's head ached a lot more now. He was rather disappointed that he didn't remember meeting Gypsy, because she seemed to be a very pretty mouse, and Sam was sure he would have liked to meet her. Or would like to have remembered meeting her. Sam was sure he would remember offering to let any mouse to use his nest. After all you didn't let just anybody stay in your nest. But here she was, and Sam wasn't sure at all as to what he should do or say next. He cast his mind back over all the polite things his mother had taught him to say and do, and nothing really seemed to cover such a situation.

"Can I get you a cup of tea?" he asked, because offering tea seemed to be the most harmless thing he could say.

"Oh, that would be lovely, but I don't want to trouble you."

"Oh no, no trouble at all, my pleasure."

#

"You see Sam, there has been no cat in the house for some time. Your grandfather was the last mouse to actually fight and defeat a cat. We mice have been very lucky since then."

Gypsy took a sip of tea and nibbled on a piece of bread that Sam had found, still unspoiled from last night's activities.

Sam had quickly tidied his apartment, with a little help from Gypsy, and now they sat in his kitchen having a late breakfast. Sam's headache was going away, but he was still torn between wanting to get to know Gypsy better and hoping she would leave quickly so he could go back to sleep. Sudden flashes of anxiety about his task to defeat the cat intruded between those two thoughts, but as that seemed very unreal at the moment, the anxiety was like a stabbing pain. There for a moment, but quickly gone.

"I'm sure you know more about it than I do, but my friends on the committee tell me that whilst no house mouse has been killed, several of the *field mice,"* Gypsy paused, and screwed her nose up. "Several of the poor field mice have been killed while foraging for food in the pantry and kitchen."

Sam tutted some sympathy. He hadn't had much to do with the field mice, but he didn't like the idea of any mouse being killed. Especially by a cat.

"Anyway," Gypsy continued, "I'm sure I don't need to tell you how to do your business, after all you are the expert on this whole cat and mouse business." Gypsy leaned forward and touched him on the arm. "But, Sam, I do know that something needs to be done. I don't know you well Sam, but from what I have heard..." Gypsy looked down, as if embarrassed, "and seen, I do think you are probably the only hope the mice have..."

She looked back up at him. Sam noticed how beautiful her eyes were. He rather thought that he would fight three cats right then and there if she would only look at him with those eyes for a little bit longer.

Chapter Three - How To Kill A Cat

Sam sat in his favorite chair. Although now that he had slept in it all night, it didn't seem as comfortable as it usually did. The more he thought about it, the more he realized that he may very well be the right mouse to deal with this cat. It had indeed been some time since the mice had been troubled by a cat. Most mice had completely forgotten how dangerous a cat could be. But Sam was right in the middle of writing a book about his grandfather, Noah, which did make him somewhat of an expert on cats, and fighting cats. Sam's grandfather had spent hours telling Sam all about the cat, how it had terrorized the mice, how the mice had gone hungry because nobody could go into the kitchen to get food. Sam had thought it sounded terrible, all these hungry mice, their parents going searching for food, sometimes never coming back.

Grandfather was a wonderful story teller, and sometimes he almost made Sam cry when he heard about the hungry orphaned mice. Sam's heart would race with excitement and a touch of fear, when his Grandfather would get up and pace around the room, just like a cat would. When he got to a really exciting part in the story, Grandfather would pounce towards Sam, like a cat pouncing on a poor mouse, making him gasp with fear, and then giggle with relief. But after

Sam's own encounter with the cat, his Grandfather had stopped telling cat stories. Even though Grandfather had defeated the cat, he would only look at Sam and give him a rough affectionate rub on his head and say, "Ahh, Sam, the cats gone, he won't bother you again." Sometimes he would say, "But at what cost. At what cost?" But he would never say any more to Sam about the cat.

Sam had loved those stories, and even more, he had loved the time he had spent with his grandfather, and he missed him dearly. Despite being a born story teller and a mouse that was very well travelled, Sam's grandfather hadn't had many close friends among the mice. From his stories, Sam knew that he had made friends with all manner of creatures, including, if he was to be believed, and Sam did believe, a barn owl. How a mouse became friends with a barn owl is a story he never told, but it must have been quite a story.

One day, not long after Sam had become an independent young mouse, with a nest of his own, his grandfather had come to see him. They had played a game of chess, and Sam had beat his grandfather with some very easy moves. Something that had never happened before. They had shared some cheese and some very fine wine.

"Sam," his grandfather had said after a long moment of companionable silence. "This place has many memories for me. Some good. Some not so good," Sam had glanced around his nest, not understanding.

"I don't like a lot of what I see around me these days. I've seen things I created be twisted into things I hate. Many of the mice I truly care about are gone now. You are all that keeps me here. Keeps me from going of exploring again. But you've come of age now, you've grown into a fine young mouse and now, I think it's time for me to go into the world and explore some more."

Sam had protested. Questioned. But to no avail. His grandfather had said he would "be back in a while to tell some more stories..." But he never did come back, and by now he would be a very very old mouse. Sam still hoped that one day his grandfather would drop by, and share some cheese, beat Sam at chess and then tell a story of his adventures. But as each day passed, Sam knew this was less and less likely.

After his grandfather had gone, Sam started to realize that even though he was the greatest influence on Sam's life, Sam didn't know much about his grandfather. He knew lots of stories about his adventures. But not much else. What Sam did know, was that he wanted to tell stories too. Just like his Grandfather.

So Sam decided he would be a writer and that he would rather like to write a book. Being an author seemed like quite a grand thing, and something for which he would be proud to tell all his friends, and something he thought his grandfather would be quite proud of as well. Sam had decided that his first book would be about his Grandfather.

"How's your book going?" his friends would ask.

"Just gathering details. Background reading, research. You know how it is when you are writing a book," Sam would say. And his friends would nod, for none of them had ever written a book and this seemed entirely the proper way to go about writing a book.

"Today," Sam said, to himself, because research is solitary affair and speaking out loud broke the silence and made him feel less lonely, "I shall re-read my notes on Grandfather Noah and come up with a strategy."

#

Sam drank several cups of tea whilst re-reading all his notes. He'd also had some cheese. Hard cheddar, which always seemed to be the best kind of cheese for research. The soft cheeses seemed to be all together too lazy for writing, and definitely too indulgent for research. Tea and hard cheese. This seemed, to Sam, to be the best combination for research.

Sam had moved from his comfortable chair to his desk, because he had found himself nodding off to sleep after his rather late night of partying. His chair also smelt faintly of Gypsy, and he had found himself day-dreaming about her delicate whiskers and her soft brown eyes. He thought about the way she had looked at him when she spoke about how brave she thought Sam was.

A single page was sitting in his typewriter, and Sam sat staring at this piece of paper. It was a nice clean piece of paper. A slight cream color. He had typed a two-word heading, and because it was important, had underlined it.

There hadn't been a lot of information in his notes. Not that Sam could find anyway, and he found that, whilst he had kept his desk very tidy, and had categorized, annotated, flagged and cross referenced all his research, he still couldn't find out much about HOW you actually fought a cat. There was a lot of background information on cats. There was also a lot about who his grandfather was, and some famous things that his grandfather had said. Sam had even interviewed some good mice who had known his grandfather. Sam had actually gone so far as to write some rather well written (or so he thought) rough drafts of the chapters concerning his grandfather's early life.

But there was not much information on how his grandfather had actually defeated the cat. In fact, now that Sam had started looking, he couldn't actually find a description of the final, famous, moment when, apparently Grandfather Noah had called the cat out, in the kitchen, and told the cat, in thunderous tones that, "Not one more mouse shall die on your vile claws."(at least according to an interview Sam had conducted, with a mouse who hadn't actually been there, but had heard about it later.)

This struck Sam as rather inconvenient, and evidence that he still needed to gather a lot more research before he could write his book.

Or fight the cat.

It then struck Sam that if he didn't figure out how to defeat the cat, he might not get the chance to write his book. This disturbed Sam, for his whole life he had considered himself to be a writer, and the thought of not completing even one book was very alarming indeed.

"An Action plan. That's what I need. Grandfather always said that the cheese doesn't come to he who waits. The cheese goes to those who take action."

So, with a very decisive frame of mind, Sam had placed a piece of paper into the typewriter and typed out the first heading. He sat and looked at the piece of paper.

ACTION PLAN

But Sam had got stuck at this point, and wasn't sure what else he should do. More research indeed. But Sam wasn't sure where to even start writing an action plan. Not an action plan for defeating a cat anyway. He had written many action plans on writing his book. Some very good action plans. He stared at the paper. And stared. But no ideas came to him.

There was a sharp knock at the door. At almost that exact moment his headache seemed to reappear. Sam had hoped that there would be no more interruptions today. The letter from the committee arriving, then members of the committee themselves arriving, a party and having a guest stay for breakfast had all taken a large amount of time and energy. Not to mention the fact that now instead of writing his book, Sam needed to research how to fight a cat, and then, when he had completed that research, he would have to... well, he would have to fight a cat.

The sharp knock at the door was repeated.

"Yes, yes, I'm coming," Sam said.

A third sharp knock.

He swung open his front door. There standing in the door, bold as you please was the rather dapper looking mouse from the party last night. Sam's headache got a touch worse. Behind the Dapper Mouse, who's name Sam struggled to recall, lurked the rattish looking mouse, also from his party last night. Sam frowned to himself. The Rattish mouse scowled back. Much to his frustration, Sam couldn't remember the names of either mouse.

"Morning Sam, old chap," Dapper Mouse said.

Rattish just continued scowling at him.

"Committee would like a word with you Sam, don't want to interrupt, what with your important preparations and all, but they thought they should get a brief… an update, as it were, on what you are planning. They don't like surprises, the committee," said Dapper Mouse.

"Err… well, umm, I can probably tidy up things here and come later.. I mean, I was just finishing, well not quite finishing, starting perhaps. Starting my action plan. Shall I complete it before seeing the committee? Perhaps I should prepare a brief, or a presentation for the committee first?" Sam asked.

"The Committee wants to see you now," said Rattish Mouse. It was the first time Sam had heard Rattish Mouse speak. He had quite a gruff voice.

"I'll just get my things shall I? I need to get my action plan," Sam said, his mouth a little bit dry, for he knew that his action plan had no action, nor any plan in it. And action plan with no action, nor plan isn't really anything.

"Don't need things. Don't need an action plan. You need action. Plans and Action don't go together," growled Rattish Mouse. Rattish Mouse pulled Sam out of his doorway, closed it behind him and gave Sam a firm push down the hall towards the Town Hall.

"Err, I need to take my action plan," said Sam.

"You either plan, or you act. Tell the committee what you are going to do about the cat. No action plan needed, just action." said Rattish Mouse.

With Rattish mouse on one side, and Dapper Mouse on the other, Sam walked towards the committee meeting.

Chapter Four - A Task Is Set

Sam sat outside the committee's meeting room. The bench was very hard. The door to the committee's meeting chamber was very thick and ornate. It looked like a proper door for such an important group of mice. Sam could hear mutterings from within. Sometimes hushed, and sometimes loud, but always, Sam could tell, important. Sam wondered what it was that the committee was discussing, and why they were taking so long.

Dapper Mouse had gone inside and had not come back out. Rattish Mouse stood by the doorway, as if to stop Sam running away. Sam smiled at Rattish Mouse. Rattish Mouse stared at him.

"Roland," Rattish Mouse said.

"Er, what? Roll what?" Sam said.

"Roland. My name is Roland."

"Nice to meet you Mr Roland. My name is Sam."

"I know that already," said Roland.

"Damon." Roland said.

"Damon?" asked Sam, not sure what Roland was talking about.

"The other fellow. The well dressed mouse. His name is Damon. He works for the committee. No one introduced us last night, too busy being polite and well mannered. But I thought you might like to know our names."

Sam was about to ask what Roland did for the committee when the door to the committee room opened. For such a big door, it opened very quietly. Damon leaned out, a cheerful smile on his face.

"Hey ho Sam, the committee is ready for you now. Don't be nervous. Just the key points on how you are going to deal with the cat. They trust you on the detail." Sam smiled back, feeling very nervous as he stood up and walked inside the committee room.

Sam had never been inside the committee room before. Like most mice he didn't really know what the committee did, other than make sure that the interests of mice and affiliated rodents were looked after. And a fine job they did, Sam was sure, because he had quite a comfortable life, and until now, it had been quite uneventful. And if a mouse could live a quiet and uneventful life, then surely the committee was doing its job.

The committee room was magnificent. There were very nice dark wood panels on all the walls. Sam glanced around. The room felt *important*. It looked very much like the proper place to talk about important things. Things that needed to be talked about by important people. Sam wondered if his words would sound silly in such an important place.

Paintings of past committee members were on all the walls, and to his surprise, Sam noticed a painting of his grandfather. A small brass plaque was under the painting, but Sam couldn't read it from where he stood in the doorway. Sam had not known that there was a painting of his grandfather. He very much wanted to have a closer look. A copy of it might even make a good cover for his book… When he finished writing it.

"Do go in Sam," said Dapper Mouse. "Go and stand before the dais. The committee won't bite." Dapper gave him another little push into the room. Sam felt Roland hulking behind him, closing the door.

"Come, come." A voice boomed from the platform at the end of the room. "We don't have all day. Come and tell us about what you are going to do about the cat."

The booming voice startled Sam. It was the old mouse from the party. The one who had fallen asleep in his arm chair. He was glaring at Sam quite gruffly, and pointing to a spot in the center of the room. Sam walked to the middle of the room. There were some chairs behind him, probably for spectators, Sam thought, although he had never thought that anyone would be interested in sitting in on a committee meeting. It would be terribly dry stuff. Or terribly important and confidential. Either way, it had never entered Sam's head that a mouse would care to sit in on a meeting of the committee.

In front of Sam, the committee sat in a row. Each of the members had their own desk, and the desks were quite high, so that the committee members were higher than Sam, even though he was standing. The Mayor sat in the center, and on one side was Mr. Montagu and on the other side was the old mouse that had been at his apartment, still glaring at him. There were several other mice that Sam didn't recognize.

It occurred to Sam that he didn't really know many of the committee members at all. The Mayor, certainly he knew the Mayor. But not to talk to. They must be too busy with important committee work to really get out and meet other mice. But they looked like very wise and important mice, and Sam realized how much responsibility they had placed in him by selecting him to deal with the cat.

Sam stood still, flushed with nervousness and excitement. He still didn't know what he was going to do about the cat, but he felt a bit more confident that the committee would have some ideas to help him. It was quiet for a moment. Sam wasn't sure what one did when standing in front of the committee. He glanced over at the painting of his grandfather, hoping that this would give him inspiration.

"All the paintings in this room are of committee members," said Mr Montagu. "The most important mice ever to live are on these walls."

"Oh," said Sam.

"Your grandfather is the only mouse to have his painting on these walls who wasn't a committee member. That's how highly we think of your grandfather," Mr Montagu continued.

"Oh," said Sam again, not sure what else to say.

"I'm sure that you can have a closer look at the painting at some later stage. I dare say you would like to include a copy of the painting in your book? It would make a very good cover wouldn't it? Once this cat business is finished, I believe the committee would be happy to let you come here and have a look.

"Maybe we might give you access to the committee's library and the archives. All the important records are in there. Probably a lot of information that would be of great use for your book." Mr Montagu glanced at the other committee members who all nodded or shrugged.

"I'd say the committee wants the cat dealt with as a priority before we talk about anything else," said the Mayor.

"Of course," said Mr Montagu. "Sam, I'm the committee member for Food and Supplies. That makes the cat my problem. The cat is my problem, because we mice need to be able to gather food and supplies, and the presence of a cat makes that job very difficult indeed. I don't need to tell you, of all people about how risky food gathering is. We know you lost your parents when you were a pup. We know that your mother and father were killed by this very same cat."

Sam closed his eyes. For a moment he was a pup again, on his first forage by himself.

Mr Montagu cleared his throat.

"As I was saying, the committee knows full well the sacrifices your parents made. After you were rescued by your grandfather, when your parents were killed, your grandfathers resolved to the committee that he would make the house safe for all mice. And he did. Your grandfather helped the committee come up with a very good plan for making sure that no house mouse would ever be a victim of the cat again. Your parents were the last *house mice* to fall victim to the cat."

"So you see Sam," the Mayor took over. "Poor Mr Charles Montagu. His job is to make sure that every mouse gets a fair share of the food. And with your Grandfathers help in setting up our foraging system, we've had a very fair distribution of food. No more foraging for the average house mouse. In return for shelter in the house, the field mice forage for everyone, so thanks to the help of the field mice, no more foraging and no more cat.

"Except now. The cat has returned. Several field mice have been killed by this terrible beast, and that has made foraging hard. And that simply cannot be tolerated."

The old mouse sat up. "*Field mice.* Poor wretched creatures. There are so many of them, that a few here and there don't matter, poor wee beasties. Maybe we should have left them in the fields where they belong." He slumped back down and muttered something that Sam couldn't quite hear.

"Hmm… yes Winston, we all know how you feel about the whole field mouse situation," the Mayor said, frowning at the old mouse. Looking back at Sam, he continued

"Sam, the food store is starting to get smaller, which makes us worry. You may have noticed that your grocery deliveries are getting a bit less frequent?" Sam hadn't actually noticed, although he had known that Gruyere was a bit hard to come by lately, but that's what makes a good cheese so delightful. You can't always get it.

"So," the Mayor said, "we know you probably have some research to do, some plans, maybe a bit of training to prepare yourself hmm? But we want you to understand that this is a serious matter. Not some adventurous lark to impress the ladies. Mice are dying and something needs to be done about it Sam. And it effects not just those mice foraging, but everyone, for if our food stops, then all mice will need to spend their days foraging, and that's hardly a civilized way for mice to live.

"We know you have suffered more than many, but we also know that the blood of your grandfather and your father runs in you. If anybody understands how important this is, then it is you. The committee believes in you, and you have our full support in this terribly important matter. You may have met young Gypsy at your apartment last night? Yes?"

Sam nodded, his heart skipping a beat as he remembered watching her nibble on a piece of cheese.

"She will be your liaison with the committee. If you need to speak to us, or if we need to speak to you, let her know. She will help you with your day to day plans."

Sam suddenly felt a little bit brighter.

"Is there anything you need from the committee to help you?" the mayor asked, in a tone that suggested that the meeting was finishing up.

"Well, your honour... er, I mean, Mr Mayor, as you may know I was writing a book on my Grandfather, and well, my research has sort of failed to uncover *how* he actually fought and defeated the cat. I was wondering if the committee knows of any mouse who might have been fortunate enough to have witnessed the fight? It might help me to finish my action plan if I could, well, you know, speak to such a mouse."

"I don't believe there is any mouse who actually witnessed that great battle, so I don't think we can help you," the Mayor said, looking at the other committee members, who all nodded in agreement, except for Winston, the old grey mouse.

Winston sat up and looked directly at Sam. The Mayor frowned. Winston's eyes were watery and his fur grey, but Sam realized that he was still very much an alert and cunning old mouse.

"It is well that you aren't going to fly off without any planning or research. There were no mice who witnessed the battle, but your grandfather was an odd fellow for a mouse. He had many friends other than house mice. Kept strange company, he did. You might want to speak to the rats, he spent some time with the rats, strange as that may sound. But mind you take care if you seek out the rats. They are a strange breed, not altogether friendly, and don't suffer fools lightly." Winston slide his glasses down on his nose and sat back closing his eyes again. "Good luck."

The Mayor banged his gavel, and the committee all stood up and started walking out a side door. The door swung open, held open by Damon. Sam left the committee room, his mind a whirl. *Rats,* Sam thought. They scared him even more than cats. At least you knew where you stood with a cat. But rats...they were unpredictable and dangerous.

"Hello."

Sam jumped. Roland stood next to the door, smiling at Sam, his rather large teeth glistening. Sam's heart skipped a beat. Sam looked around and noticed that the door was closed, and that Damon had gone back inside. There was no other mouse around, and the foyer seemed rather gloomy and quiet. He rather thought that Roland looked far more rattish at the moment than mouse like.

"Good meeting was it?" said Roland. He grabbed Sam's arm tightly.

"Let's walk and talk. You and me."

Roland relaxed his grip as they walked. He didn't seem in any hurry, but Sam tried to walk a bit faster. He very much wanted to get to some of the passage ways where there were other mice, scurrying around their daily business. He didn't think Roland was going to hurt him, but at the same time, he did look a *lot* like a rat, and that made Sam quite nervous, in a way that Sam found hard to explain.

"I can take you to meet King Rat," said Roland.

"Why would I want to meet King Rat?" Sam asked, his voice squeakier than he would like.

"Because he knew your grandfather quite well. They were friends, in a way," said Roland. "King Rat rather admired your grandfather. And your grandfather trusted him quite a bit. They used to play chess."

"Oh," said Sam. "Er… well, perhaps, I could write down some questions for him, a written interview perhaps?"

"I don't think that will do. You see," said Roland leaning forward and smiling, showing his big white teeth, "King Rat wants to meet you."

Chapter Five - Research

Sam sat back at his desk at his typewriter, still with just a single piece of paper in it, titled Action Plan. The idea of an action plan seemed both incredibly important and now, somewhat silly. It seemed that action was happening to him, without any plan. If only the world would leave him alone for long enough to write his action plan.

Roland had walked him back to his home. Other than telling Sam that he would 'arrange a meeting' with King Rat, Roland hadn't said much more. He had ignored Sam's questions. His final words to Sam were "Don't tell anyone that you are meeting King Rat. It might not be good for you." He'd closed Sam's door, only to open it again, startling Sam yet again."Oh..I hope you like chess. King Rat likes chess."

Sam tried couldn't work out how, or where his world had become so complicated. Cats! Rats! The Committee! Gypsy.

Sam smiled, well, at least that was one very nice thing. He'd spent so much time lately writing and researching his book that he had hardly spent any time in the company of other mice. He was rather looking forward to seeing Gypsy again.

Still, he thought *I must work on my plan. I can't fly off without any plan. Hmm, fly off.* The thought of flying tickled Sam's thoughts a little bit. *I think I should visit Sugar Glider. He always has a plan for everything he does. And he always takes action too!*

Sam had come to know Sugar Glider quite by accident when he was researching his grandfathers past. After his grandfather had become a hero for defeating the cat, he had taken to disappearing for hours on end. Sam had asked around the older mice who knew him "Quite odd," one had said "He used to go up to the attic a lot. Just sat out on a small ledge there, staring off into the fields, and at the lake beyond. Never said why he went there. Damm fool thing if you ask me, a mouse has no business sitting high on a ledge where a hawk could swoop down and get him. Still, who am I to question the actions of a mouse that is brave enough to have fought a cat?"

Sam hadn't found any mouse that could explain why his grandfather used to go up to the attic, so one day he had taken the long journey up there himself. It had taken all his nerve to step out onto the ledge. The wind was blowing gently, ruffling Sam's fur slightly, but it felt like a gale. Sam had looked down and almost fainted when he saw how high he was. Down below he could see the grass of the back yard, and his stomach did a kind of back flip when he thought about falling. There was the branch of an ancient oak tree close enough to touch. Sam forced himself to look around, to try to see what it was that his grandfather saw when he came here.

Beyond the wide unkempt grass of the back-yard was a field of long lush grass, and then a forest, and in the distance Sam had seen glistening water, a lake or a river, sparkling through the soft green of the trees.

"Hullo. Who are you then?" A gentle, cheerful voice had called out from behind the greenery of the oak tree. Sam had startled and almost fallen off the ledge. If it was a hawk he wouldn't have heard a thing, just the sound of wind through feathers and the feel of sharp claws.

A soft gentle face had peered out of the foliage.

"I'm Sugar Glider!" it said, a small paw had extending out beyond the foliage. Sam had stared at if for a moment before realising that he should shake it.

"Hello Mr Glider, I'm Sam."

As Sam had shaken paws with Sugar Glider, he had noticed that Sugar Glider had a long flap of skin going from his front paws to his back paws, that looked rather like a wing. Sam had heard of Sugar Gliders, but didn't really know what they were. He thought they were some sort of squirrel or possum, but onc that could glide by jumping from tree to tree. "Do you use those to fly?" Sam had asked, pointing to the flap of skin.

"Glide." Sugar glider had said. "I don't fly. I'm not a bird. I glide. Much harder."

That had been the start of an odd, but very close friendship. Sam didn't even realise it himself, but Sugar Glider was probably Sam's best friend. Sugar Glider was certainly the most cheerful and happy animal that Sam had ever met. Nothing seemed to get Sugar Glider down, and despite the long climb to the attic, and the nervousness Sam felt whenever he climbed out on the ledge, Sam had come to spend a lot of time up there, at first on the ledge, and later, climbing out onto the oak tree. Just sitting and talking to Sugar Glider.

Well, thought Sam, his thoughts returning to the task at hand, *at least I've got some time now to have a cup of tea and get some rest.* Sam's nose twitched with delight as the aroma of his favorite tea drifted up to his nose. *I might sit in bed, drink my tea and have an early night. I think I shall go and see Sugar Glider in the morning and see what he has to say.*

Suddenly there was a sharp knock at the door. So sudden that Sam spilt his tea on the floor, and some of it splashed onto his toes.

"What NOW?" Sam cried out. "My nerves are almost gone with all these interruptions!"

Sam opened the door ready to yell 'Go Away!' to whoever it was that was disturbing him.

But he stopped himself just in time, his anger melting away and despite himself he felt a warm glow creeping across his face.

"Hello Sam." said Gypsy. Sam was very happy to see Gypsy, but she didn't seem happy at all. In fact, she looked quite distraught. Her nose was twitching, and it looked to Sam like she might cry. Her eyes seemed to be filling with tears. Sam hoped she wouldn't cry, but straight away he wanted to put his arms around her and tell her that no matter what was wrong, he would look after her.

"Oh Sam," she said. "It's terrible. The cat is in the kitchen and its trapped some mice. You must come right away. You must. I don't know who else can save them."

Chapter Six - Confronting the Cat

Sam peered through a crack in the skirting board. In the centre of the kitchen, a large orange cat paced back and forth. The cat's head turned slowly from side to side, scanning the entire kitchen. Every now and then Sam saw a flash of the cat's green eyes, and he felt butterflies in his stomach. Memories of being caught in the gaze of those evil green eyes as a pup raced through his mind. Even though the crack was very tiny, and the passage way behind the skirting board was quite dimly lit behind the skirting board, Sam felt sure that the cat could see him sitting there. The cat stared at the crack for a moment, and licked its lips with a sly smile. Sam felt his body freezing up. He couldn't move. Then the cat continued slowly and casually patrolling around the kitchen floor. Stopping every now and then to hiss and mutter under its breathe.

"What should we do?" Gypsy whispered into his ear.

"Er… I don't think we should do anything at the moment," Sam said. "There doesn't seem to be any mouse in danger, and we haven't really got a plan to deal with the cat just yet."

In the gloomy passageway Sam could just make out Gypsy's outline. She nodded and looked back out at the pacing cat. "Something's got him worked up. It looks like he is after something, I don't know where the pups went," Gypsy said.

"We're quite safe here behind the skirting board. I don't think he knows we are here."

A field mouse came running down the passage way, skidding to a stop in front of them.

"The cat," he said panting. "The cat is out there."

"Yes, we know," said Gypsy. "We were watching him before you disturbed us."

"But there are mice in the pantry...Michelle took them out for a forage... They've been trapped by the cat," said the field mouse, sounding a little bit panicked.

"Look here, young fellow, calm down, what's your name?" Sam asked.

"George," the young mouse said, catching his breath. "I was on look out for the foraging party when I saw the cat, but the foragers had all gone into the pantry, so I couldn't warn them. They are going to get eaten and I couldn't stop them. They are only pups."

"Pups?" said Sam. "Why would you teach pups about foraging when the cat is around?" Sam asked.

Poor pups. Trapped inside the pantry. It must be terrifying for them. At least they are safe inside the pantry. Not trapped under a chair. Sam stopped himself from thinking about being trapped by the cat, otherwise he would freeze up again.

"Not teaching about foraging, they are foraging. Pups forage once they are weaned," said George.

"Why? Why would you send out such young pups to forage?" said Sam. "Look what you've done. Now they are caught in the pantry and who knows how long it will be before the cat looses interest? Why didn't their parents check the area first?"

"They are from the orphanage. They don't HAVE parents mister. If we don't forage, we don't eat."

"Of course you can eat," said Sam. "Everyone gets food. Even with a cat around, there is enough food for everyone. What do you think the committee does? It manages our food. Or do you send them out to get extra food for yourself?" Sam was almost yelling at George, his anger rising again.

George glared at Sam. "Where do you think your food comes from Mr House Mouse? Who do you think gets your food? " George shouted.

"Shush, shush," Gypsy said, patting Sam gently on the back. "Let's not worry about it now. Something needs to be done about the pups. Sam, isn't there anything you can do?" Gypsy looked at him with her beautiful brown eyes.

Sam looked back through the crack in the skirting board. His heart gave a jump. A pair of big green eyes was staring right into the crack. Straight at him. Sam knew those big green eyes. It was the same big green eyes that had stared at him when he was a pup, trapped under the chair.

"Look," Gypsy whispered. "Some of the pups are making a run for it."

Sam forced himself to look past the cats piercing eyes. One of the pups, taking advantage of the distracted cat was dashing across the floor, trying to reach a hole in the skirting board on the far side of the kitchen.

No. Sam thought. *Not yet. Its not safe. That cat is fast and cunning. Go back. Please please please go back.* But they didn't. Several more pups followed. But the cat, with that strange sense for which cats are famous, must have heard the pitter-patter of the pup's feet across the kitchen tiles, for the cat, smiled, showing razor sharp teeth, and turned to look at the pups dashing across the floor.

The first pup was almost at the hole, but three of the other pups were in the middle of the floor.

"They'll never make it," Gypsy whispered, her voice dry and raspy.

"Hey you," Sam shouted, and started kicking the inside of the skirting board. George looked at Sam like he was crazy, but then started yelling and kicking as well. The cat turned back and glanced at the skirting board for a moment, but then shrugged and turned back towards the pups standing out in the open.

But the distraction was enough for the first pup to make it into the hole. Sam sighed with relief as he saw a tail disappearing into the darkness of the hole. But fear gripped him again when he looked around and saw that the other three pups had run under the shadow of a kitchen chair. And stopped. Stopped under the very kitchen chair where Sam had taken shelter so long ago.

The cat was lying down in a crouch, its legs tense, ready to pounce, creeping forward towards the chair, slowly but with playful confidence. Sam could see its big fat tail, twitching slowly from side-to-side. The pups were frozen still, mesmerized by the big green eyes and the slowly twitching tail.

Just like me. Sam thought. In his mind he could see that day. See the cat stalking towards him. His father had run out from the edge of the room, yelling at the cat. His mother, did the same, from the other side. His father got right up to the cats tail and almost pounced on the tail. But the cat was fast. It jumped and spun around and was on his father in a ball of hissing fur. Sam didn't remember much else. Not until his grandfather came out and led him away from the chair, holding his head tight against him so that he wouldn't look and see what the cat was doing. Sam could still remember every bit of fear and terror that had run through his body that day.

Sam closed his eyes hard. He couldn't look at those pups anymore, he couldn't look at the cat stalking them. He couldn't watch it all happen again. His whole body trembled.

Without any further thought, Sam went running along the passageway. Behind him he could hear Gypsy yelling.

"Sam, come back, Sam..."

But Sam couldn't hear her at all. All he could hear was the pounding fear in his heart.

As he ran down the passageway, the pup that had made it safely into the hole came running from the other direction. He was crying. "Mister, mister, please help," Sam ignored the pup, brushing past him and soon the pup's cries were also behind him, and the sound just made him run faster.

Sam found himself standing right at the hole in the skirting board. Looking out at the kitchen floor. Looking across the kitchen floor. Looking at three little field mouse pups. And one big orange cat. Sam ran out onto the kitchen floor. Faster than he had ever run before. So fast that his mind didn't even have time to realize what he was going to do. Because if his mind did realize what he was going to do, he surely would have skidded to a halt and ran back into the safe hole.

Sam zig zag-ed across the floor, fast. But quiet. He ran behind the cat, which was staring oh-so intently at the three little pups. He ran right next to the cat. So close he almost brushed against its long dirty orange hair. He ran to the cats long fat twitching tail. And he jumped on the tail. And he held on as tight than he had ever held on to anything.

The cat gave a loud meow of surprise. It turned its head to see what was on its tail, but as it turned its head, its tail moved. It moved away, so that cat could-n't see. The cat turned its whole body. Trying to see its tail. It turned and it turned, but it couldn't quite see its tail. Sam was being shaken. Hard. His body was banging on the kitchen floor, but he only held on even more tightly.

The cat was hissing and spinning fast. Around and around it went. But Sam stayed on. Sam didn't know what the pups were doing. He didn't know what the cats were doing. He didn't even know what he was doing.

So he just held on.

Soon the cat had spun and leapt around so much that they had moved out of the kitchen, and into the parlor. Sam's arms were getting very tired. The cat was getting tired too, and was recovering from its surprise. It gave one more violent shake of its tail, and Sam's grip gave way. He was flung off, and skidded across the floor, banging into the wall. The whole world seemed to sway around Sam, everything was moving around. Except in the center of his vision, where there was a big orange shape. An orange shape staring at him with mean green eyes. The cat hissed.

Sam stood up. He was near the door into the kitchen, and he glanced back. It was a long way, and he was exhausted, but he thought he might be able to make it back into the kitchen. Maybe. He looked back at the cat, which was glaring at him. Sam had never seen anything so angry as the glare in those nasty green eyes. The cat lowered itself, and Sam knew that in an instant the cat would pounce. Would pounce on him, and there would be no chance to run. He glanced around for somewhere to hide. But there was nowhere to go.

Instead of hissing now, the cat started purring, and its eyes glinted at him, its mouth open slightly, almost smiling at Sam, showing its razor sharp long teeth.

With a sudden and incredibly loud yowl, the cat jumped. Sam almost closed his eyes out of fear. He rolled to the side to try to get away from of the cat's pounce, but tripped on the edge of the parlor rug. He lay there waiting for the cat to land on him. But instead the cat yowled again.

Sam sat up and saw that the cat was no longer looking at him. It had its back to him, and Sam saw that there was a bright red splash of blood on the cat's tail. The cat was hissing. It leapt up onto a side table, hissing and spitting and knocking over some knick knacks.

Standing in the middle of the parlor floor was the biggest rat Sam had ever seen, not that Sam had seen many rats. He was huge, with powerful looking haunches and grey fur around his muzzle. A small drop of blood was on one of his whiskers. He looked at Sam, then back at the cat on the table, which seemed to be recovering from the surprise of being attacked twice in one day.

"Run." The rat said in a deep voice. "Run Sam. Run."

Sam ran.

Chapter Seven-Rescued

Sam stood inside the entrance to the mouse hole, still catching his breath from running all the way from the parlor. Inside the passageway there was all manner of food piled up, and the last of a chain of field mice were scampering into the hole in the wall. Sam looked in amazement at the amount of food piled up there. Sam watched as a pup struggled through the hole carrying a small bag of raisins. An adult field mouse came in behind the pup.

"That's it, last one, all the pups are home," she said, and immediately set about organizing the pups and checking if they were all right.

Sam sat back and watched the mad confusion as the mice set about moving the food into piles. Every now and then a mouse would come over and congratulate him. The house mice would pat him on the back and say things like 'well done old boy' or 'your grandpa would be proud of you, chip off the old block', and they would then mingle around and talk about how wonderful it all was, and saying to each other "Wish I'd been here, would have been right out there with Old Sam, giving that cat a dose of its own medicine."

The field mice were a bit quieter and calling him Mr Sam and thanking him, their heads bobbing gently, before going off to help with sorting the food. The whole time Gypsy stood next to him, smiling at him every time someone congratulated him, her paw resting on his arm. Sam felt quite dazed.

"Did you see the blood on that mangy old cat?" one of the house mice said. "You must have given him a fearful old chomping eh? Never knew a mouse could bite so hard."

"I didn't bite the cat..," Sam started to say,

"It was a rat."

The mice all laughed.

"Rats, " one mouse scoffed "As if a rat would involve himself in the affairs of a mice,".

"Say what you will Sam," another said, "no need to play the modest hero. That cat will think twice before messing with you again, that's for sure."

Sam started to protest, but Gypsy squeezed his arm and whispered into his ear

"Its OK Sam. It isn't often they get to meet a hero. Let them talk."

Eventually there was an even bigger commotion coming down the corridor, and the committee, lead by the Mayor turned up. The Mayor stood on a box of sardines tins, with the committee standing behind, and all the mice gathered around.

"May I be the first to congratulate Sam on his wonderful endeavors. It was only a few hours ago that Sam sought advice from the committee on how he should best deal with the cat, and already you can see the results. Thanks to the hard work and planning by the committee, we finally have hope that we may deal with the cat, and get our food supply back to where it should be. The committee will continue to work hard to ensure that this cat is dealt with."

The gathered crowd of mice all clapped. Dapper Mouse called out. "Three cheers for the Mayor. Three cheers for the committee. Hip, Hip. Hip, Hip. Hooray." All the mice called out "hooray", and the applause was a lot louder this time.

The crowd dispersed, and Sam watched as Charles Montagu gave directions for all the food to be moved to the various store houses. The Mayor and the old mouse, Winston, came over to where Sam was sitting.

"Well done Sam," the Mayor said, "but you must be sure to think of what your next step is. The cat will be much more alert now, and I fear that you have only angered him. Next time, maybe you should try something a bit more decisive. A bloody tail is a good show, but it isn't really going to defeat the cat is it? Still, at least we've got our food replenished for the time being, so some thanks are in order. " The mayor shook Sam's hand and strolled away.

Winston peered at him for a moment.

"Bloody tail eh? Never heard of a mouse doing that before. Except for your grandfather. I have heard of a rat attacking a cat. Not a mouse though." Winston turned to go, paused and they turned around to face him again. "Mice are fickle Sam. They can change their mind very quickly. Make sure you believe in yourself and disregard the opinions of those that don't matter. Your belief in yourself, your thoughts... that's all that you can ever truly call your own." He turned and strolled away.

The last of the crowd had wandered off, and Sam had begun to feel like he had recovered enough to walk home. Gypsy had left, promising to get him the tastiest morsel from the haul of food.

"Only the best cheese for the mouse of the hour. Go home and rest Sam, and I shall bring you a morsel to make your mouth water for a week," she had said.

Out of the shadows, he saw a small gathering of mice. They were all pups, except for one. Sam recognized her as the field mouse that had been the last in from the pantry.

"Hello Mr Sam," she said. "My pups would like to thank you for saving them." She gently pushed three pups towards Sam. Behind her, Sam could see over a dozen other pups hiding behind her.'

"Your Pups? They were your pups out there?" Sam felt a little bit angry. No mother should have risked all of her pups at such a young age, foraging unsupervised when there was a cat out there.

She giggled and blushed a little too. "No, they aren't *my* pups. But they are sort of my pups. These are the orphans. I look after them."

"Oh. I see," said Sam.

The three pups before him looked up and mumbled, "Thank yous", while looking at the floor.

Sam squatted down and looked them each in the eye in turn.

"You were very brave to keep calm and stay under the chair. Many mice your age would have panicked and run around, putting themselves at even more risk." One of the pups sniffed and seemed about to cry. "Don't be upset young fellow. Soon you'll be tucked up in your nest and this will all seem like a horrible dream."

Michelle smiled. "Thank you Mr Sam."

She shooed the three pups back to where the other pups stood.

"They seem very well behaved..." Sam said, catching himself before he said *"for field mice."* Because even though everyone knows that young field mice are a bit wilder, a bit less well behaved than house mice, its definitely not polite to say so. And Sam was, if nothing else, a polite mouse.

"They are good. Its not easy. I've got almost twenty orphans to look after, and its hard to give them all the attention they need. All of them have had such a hard time. Would you talk to them? It would mean a lot to them?"

Sam found himself surrounded by field mice orphans, all of them wanting to sit at his feet while he told them all about the cat. So, Sam started telling them about the rescue, and then Sam found himself telling stories about his childhood. About what it felt like being an orphan, and the things his grandfather had said and done. Many adult field mice had also gathered around, dragging over crates to sit on. Soon other field mice started arriving with pieces of bread and some hard cheese.

Some of the oldest field mice started telling stories about what it was like living in the fields, although all of them had been very young when they had left the fields to come into the house, or had heard stories from their parents, so some of the stories sounded a bit exaggerated. But then, aren't all stories a little bit exaggerated?

By the time Sam had answered all the questions and shaken all the paws and listened to all the other stories, it was getting quite late.

Sam strolled back to his apartment feeling quite happy.

#

Sam had just put the kettle on. It felt like days since he had properly sat down and had a cup of tea, and he was rather exhausted. When he had gotten home there had been a large delivery of groceries, including a particularly nice selection of cheese and fruit which had a bow around it and a little note saying 'For Sam, the mouse of the hour, Gypsy'.

Sam was just thinking about making himself a little plate for a late evening snack when there was a knock at the door. "Is there a sign out there saying 'Sam is trying to relax, please knock?'," he muttered to himself.

He opened the door, and there stood Michelle and one of the orphan pups.

"Hello Sam," she said. "I'm really sorry to intrude, I know you are probably have far more important things to worry about, but I was wondering...little Timothy here can't get to sleep, he is still quite scared of the cat."

Sam wasn't sure what he could do about that. He really didn't have any experience with pups, other than being one once himself.

Michelle leaned in and whispered "His parents were killed by the cat last week...it would mean a lot if you could reassure him. All the pups think so much of you."

"Oh, all right, come in, come in," Sam muttered, and pointed Timothy to his comfortable arm chair. "Right then, lets see," Sam said, kneeling down in front of Timothy. "There really isn't anything to be scared of. The cat can't get you now. We've got plenty of food, so you won't need to go foraging again until you are much older anyway."

Timothy's eyes started to water.

"Look, I know it was all a bit of a shock, but you aren't under the chair anymore, you are safe in the burrow and you can snuggle down with your friends and get a good night's sleep."

Timothy nodded, but there were tears running down his cheeks. Sam felt a bit awkward.

"Its not the cat..," said Timothy. "I can't stop thinking of my parents. I didn't help them. When the cat came. When he took them. I just sat there. They wouldn't have been even out foraging if it weren't for me. Its my fault. Its all my fault."

Sam remembered that awful moment when he was a pup. Glued to the ground. Frozen while the cat stalked his father and then his mother. A wave of shame and embarrassment swept over him. Sam sat up on the chair with Timothy and hugged him close. He didn't say anything. He didn't know anything he could say. Sam didn't even realize he was crying himself until Timothy reached up and wiped Sam's tears away with his paw.

"Its Ok Mr Sam."

Sam sat in the chair next to Timmy and hugged him close. He could feel Timothy's heart beating fast, and then slowing, and after a little while Timothy fell asleep. Sam gently got out of the couch and went into the kitchen where he found Michelle.

"Poor fellow has been through a lot," he said.

She nodded.

"Thank you Sam, he was so scared and they all look up to you so much. The other orphans will treat him like a little hero when he tells them he actually visited your house and you spoke to him."

"Can I make you something to eat?" Sam asked.

"Oh, no. Please, I can't trouble you any more than we already have," said Michelle. But Sam made them up a plate of cheese and a cup of tea each anyway. Her eyes were wide at the selection of cheeses and fruit that Sam put in front of them.

"So many varieties. I don't even know what half of this is," she said, and then blushed.

"Oh," said Sam feeling embarrassed himself, and hoping he hadn't offended Michelle. "I rather forgot that field mice don't like fancy cheese. I have some plain cheddar if you would prefer?"

Michelle went red, but she didn't look embarrassed this time.

"Is that what you think Sam? That we *field mice* don't *like* fancy cheese? Really?"

"Er… well, its...it's what I've been told..," Sam trailed off.

"Do you also think that we don't need as much food as a house mouse? Do you also think that we don't love our pups as much as a house mouse? Do you also think that we like to live in a smaller burrow, all crammed in together? Is that what you think?

"Because I've heard ALL of that from house mice before. I've got news for you Sam. Just because you house mice let us live in the house, it doesn't mean that you should act like you are so much better than us."

Michelle marched off into the lounge room, scooped Timothy up in her arms and stormed off. Before she got to his door there was another knock. Without asking Sam, she swung the door open and glared. The Mayor and Gypsy stood at the door.

"Well," said Gypsy, looking at Michelle then at Sam. Michelle pushed past Gypsy and the Mayor without a word and marched down the corridor.

"What's that about then Sam? I know the field mice think you are a bit of a hero, but probably doesn't pay to get too close to them you know? People might think you a bit odd. Might think you are playing up to being the hero. A word to the wise Sam, the field mice aren't like us at all. Doesn't pay to become too close to them."

The Mayor and Gypsy came in without waiting for an invitation from Sam. Gypsy glared at Sam, but the Mayor sat down and started helping himself to the plate of food that Sam had prepared earlier.

"Sam," the Mayor continued, crumbs of cheese still in his mouth. "The field mice are very much like children. They mean well, but they don't know how to behave properly. Not their fault really, not that long ago they were living in the fields. Not really house trained. You need to remember that when dealing with them."

"Spoilt children if you ask me," muttered Gypsy. "Come into our house and share our food. Then complain when they have to do a bit of work."

"Yes. Quite," said the Mayor. "Look Sam, your grandfather is part of the reason the field mice are in the house. You are too young to remember, but not long after your parents were killed, there was a terrible winter. There was plenty of food available, although the cat was still plaguing us at the time. Your grandfather heard of the plight of the field mice. They were starving. Not a morsel of food in the fields for them. So he invited them in. There was a lot of debate by the committee on the whole thing. Not everyone agreed with your grandfather, but he was very persuasive."

The mayor paused to nibble on piece of cheese. He peered into an empty tea cup and raised his eyebrow at Sam.

"I'll make a fresh pot," said Sam.

"Good chap. Anyway. As I was saying, your grandfather spent a lot of time convincing the committee that we should help out the field mice. They being affiliated rodents. One for all, all for one. You know, that sort of thing.

"Can't say its been a total success. They don't really fit in with our society. Not really like us you know? Don't have the same manners. Not a very good work ethic either. You'd be surprised how often I get a *delegation* from the field mice, complaining about something or other 'we don't have enough food' or 'the cat killed another field mouse today'. Drives me to distraction really."

"Its not like things would be easy for them if they were in fields where they belong," said Gypsy. "They complain about the cat, but in the field there would be hawks and other nasty animals to worry about. As to food...they should be happy they can forage in a fully stocked larder. Otherwise they would be eating grass seeds and living in some muddy hole in the ground. They should really go back to where they came from."

Gypsy shuddered and sat down. Next to Sam. She smiled at him.

The Mayor frowned at Gypsy. "Well, we don't really want them to leave do we Gypsy? Be a bit awkward if they left now wouldn't it?" Gypsy nodded in agreement.

"Look Sam" she continued. "The field mice think your grandfather was a hero. Now they see you as a hero. The cat has been preying on them when they forage, and they are really looking to you to solve their problem," Gypsy put her arm on Sam's and smiled. Sam felt a little bit better.

"As Gypsy says, the committee sees a lot of po-tential in you Sam, and all the mice look up to you. The thing is Sam" the Mayor continued, "The commit-tee is under a lot of pressure to deal with a number of issues. This whole cat thing is the one that has every-one's attention. The field mice are starting to make a lot of complaints about it, and once a group gets it into their head that they want to complain, they'll complain about everything. You know what good work the committee does. Would you see all of that lost because of a few complaints over a cat?

"So, we must be seen to take action on this cat business. A lot of mice are expecting great things from you. Your grandfather, were he still around, would be very proud of you, but he would also expect you to finish the job.

"Anyway, I think I will call it a night. Its been a very long day. Sam, I hope I answered all of your questions." The mayor finished up his cup of tea and got up to go.

Sam realized that he hadn't really asked any questions.

"Well, Mr Mayor I do have some questions, er… some more questions that is" Sam said.

"No, no, young fellow, I must be going. Gypsy, you'll stay for a bit won't you? Perhaps answer some of Sam's questions, if he indeed has any?"

"Of course. Sam, do you mind if I stay a little bit longer?" Gypsy said, smiling at Sam. Sam didn't mind at all.

Later, after Gypsy left, Sam realized that he didn't actually ask Gypsy any question either. At least not any questions about how the committee thought Sam should go about fighting the cat. In fact they had spent most of the evening talking about...well, now that Sam thought about it, he couldn't really recall talking about anything important at all. He did remember Gypsy leaving, and as they stood in the door to his apartment, she leaned over and gave him a soft kiss on the cheek.

"You are very cute Sam. I do think you are perhaps the bravest mouse I've ever known. Goodnight Sam. "

This took Sam by surprise, and before he could say anything she had smiled at him and closed the door. Leaving him standing there feeling quite silly for not being able to say anything smart or wise.

#

Sam had just snuggled into bed and was about to turn out the light, when there was a very loud and determined knock at the door. A knock that couldn't be ignored.

"Oh," Sam cried. "What now?"

Sam really did feel like crying. For such a solitary mouse he was getting rather tired of all the other mice that kept visiting him, and all he really wanted was some time by himself, and it was now very late.

He got up and opened the front door. In the gloom of the night time corridor he saw a hulking figure. Roland. The door was pushed open. Sam sighed. He was so tired he almost didn't feel nervous when Roland stepped into his apartment.

"Evening Sam. You look tired. You should try to get some sleep." Roland smiled at him. Sam sighed again but didn't say anything.

"Remember I said King Rat would like to meet you? Well tomorrow night is your big day. Well, tomorrow night is your big night. Do you know where Rat Hall is? Down underneath the laundry?'

"Why does he want to see me?" Sam asked.

"Well, maybe he wants to talk to you about how tasty cat's tails are?" said Roland with a grin.

"That was King Rat? The Rat that helped me escape the cat?" Sam asked.

Roland smiled and nodded. Roland gave the air a small sniff.

"Try not to be scared." Roland said with a smile. "Rats know when a mouse is scared. Puts them into a playful mood...be better for you if King Rat took you seriously." And with that he had pulled Sam's door closed.

Sam hadn't slept too well after that. He didn't quite have nightmares, but his dreams were filled with images of green eyes, twitching tails and rats smiling at him from the gloom.

Chapter Eight Advice From a Friend

Sam stood balanced on the edge of a gutter on the second story roof. There was a gentle breeze blowing and the sky was clear. Sam looked up, for even a mouse that lives in a house knows that from the sky comes danger. Whispering wings in the shape of a hawk, or an eagle, or...any number of birds that liked to feast on mice.

"Ho there Sam, good to see you my friend, good to see you."

Sam looked up and saw the smiling face of his friend the Sugar Glider. Sugar Glider was sitting back on his haunches in the fork of a large old oak tree, nibbling on a nut. Sam made the small leap from the roof top gutter to a nearby branch, and then scurried over to where Sugar Glider sat, glancing over his shoulder as he went.

"No need to fear. The eagles do not soar near here today, and the hawks are scattered on the breeze. There is no danger today. Well," said Sugar Glider "not from those magnificent birds..."

"Hello Sugar Glider, how are you?" Sam said, pretending to not be nervous about the hawks and eagles.

"I am fine my little friend, fine indeed. I have been gliding all morning. This breeze is lovely. Consistent. Could be stronger. Could be stronger. But consistent breezes allow me to practice the same moves over and over. That's the secret at getting good at anything. Practice. Practice the same move. Over and over. And this steady breeze is good for a mornings gliding."

"I would love to be able to fly," said Sam, which was both true, and also a good way to get Sugar Glide into a conversation. If you didn't grab Sugar Gliders interest straight away, he was liable to launch himself into the breeze and fly away.

"Glide," Sugar Glider corrected. "I glide, it takes much more skill than flying. I can't just flap my wings if things go wrong, I've got to glide all the way." Sugar Glider paused and kept nibbling on the nut.

"Still, it must be a lot of fun. I wish I was you, I wish I could just fly...er, glide through the air, it must be wonderful to have that freedom. If only I could fly away, things would be so much better."

The glider stopped gnawing at the nut and looked at Sam.

"And what problems do you have that you would wish to glide away from Sam? I thought you had a rather nice life?"

"Its the cat. Well, its the cat and the committee. You see, the cat is back, and its been attacking mice. So the committee passed a resolution that something must be done."

Sugar Glider gave a little grunt. "Resolution! Passed a resolution did they. What does the cat think about that?"

Sam continued on, ignoring the interruption. "They've chosen me to deal with the cat. Its quite an honor when you think about it."

The two sat for a moment thinking about it.

"You don't sound so sure." said Sugar Glider.

"Well, I'm sure that its an honor. But I'm not sure how one does it. Defeat a cat. Everyone seems to think I know how to defeat the cat. But I can't find anything in grandfather's story that tells me how he did it. I'm going to fail at it. And other mice will think very poorly of me indeed.

"I can't even write my book now, because I don't even know how my grandfather fought the cat. So, right now, just flying away somewhere else seems very attractive. If I don't come up with a plan soon, I think the committee will be very disappointed in me."

"The committee." Sugar Glider snorted. "Mice and affiliated rodents." Sugar Glider snorted again. "A bunch of fat mice waffling on about 'Who moved my cheese?' and passing resolutions that mean nothing. You place too much trust in them Sam. They are only interested in themselves, they couldn't care a bean about mice, let alone 'affiliated rodents'."

Sam's nose twitched in disagreement. He did think that the committee was a little bit self important, but then that was the nature of people on committees, and who could question that it took important people to do important things, so perhaps it wasn't that they were self important, but that they were important selves.

"Well, they do keep the rats in check, we've had so little trouble from the rats, once the rats were allowed to be represented on the committee, and I know the food situation is a lot better since Mr Montagu has been in charge," Sam said.

Sugar Glider shrugged his shoulders and nibbled on a piece of nut he had kept in his cheeks. Sam waited. For he knew that Sugar Glider was thinking.

"Listen to me Sam," the glider said, "you can't run away from your problems. Even when you run away, your problems are still there. You will still be you, and your problems will still be yours.

"Happiness is not the absence of problems, it is the ability to deal with them. You want to build a life without problems, but that will never happen. You need to build yourself, so you can deal with your problems.

"You must face your problems square on. My longest glides are when I am gliding into the breeze, not with it. The breeze gives me lift."

"If I were someone else, then at least I wouldn't have *my* problems," said Sam, feeling a bit grumpy with Sugar Glider.

"Sam, everyone thinks they want to be someone else, and that if they were someone else, or somewhere else, then all their problems would go away. But its not true."

"What about you?" Sam said. "Not a care in the world, gliding in the morning breeze every day," Sam felt a little bit angry at Sugar Glider, even though he was his best friend. He had hoped Sugar Glider would give him more advice than just 'face your problems'.

"But that's what I mean Sam, sometimes I do wish I was someone else. You know who I want to be?"

Sam shook his head.

"I want to be a hawk." he said, and was silent, looking up at the sky. Then he whispered. "Have you ever seen them Sam? They are magnificent, they fly so fast, and so high, dancing around the thermals, and when the wind blows, they stretch their wings and soar for hours without even flapping. They are the lords of the sky Sam, they have mastered flying in a way I can only dream about, and that's what I do Sam, I dream about being a hawk, and leaving the trees, and drifting through the sky, master of the wind. Flying. Not Gliding."

Sam was silent.

"I speak to them sometimes," Sugar Glider continued. "They land in the trees...sometimes they speak back, most of the time they ignore me. I know they would eat me in a heartbeat if they could get close. But still they do talk to me. Sometimes they tell me magnificent things about flying. I've learnt a lot of things about flying from the hawks and eagles. More than any other Sugar Glider I know. Yesterday they told me all about lift and drag Sam. Lift and drag, its what makes gliding possible."

"How does that help me with MY problem," Sam interrupted, before his friend could keep talking about gliding.

"I admire the hawks Sam," Sugar Glider continued, "but that doesn't mean I really want to be one. They fly beautifully. I love their grace and control of the air. They live for themselves, and don't care about the opinions of others. I admire that about them. If I could learn just a little bit about flying from them, and if I could learn to care less about the opinions of others..." Sugar Glider trailed off and looked into the distance and then suddenly he looked at Sam. "But they are cruel, so very cruel. And as much as I can admire things about them, beyond anything, the biggest thing about the hawks is the very thing I don't want to be, and that is cruel and uncaring."

Sugar Glider said nothing. He just sat their smiling at Sam. An absent minded smile that made Sam feel like Sugar Glider had given him an answer and that Sam wasn't smart enough to understand it.

"Sugar Glider, you knew my grandfather," Sam said.

"Not well Sam, for I was just a joey when he was around, but of course I know *about* your grandfather."

"Anyway," continued Sam, "I was really wondering how my Grandfather did it, how he actually defeated the cat."

"Did your grandfather defeat the cat?" Sugar Glider asked, looking at Sam out of the corner of his eyes.

In the distance a breeze drifted in across the lake, ruffling the water, then across the forest, making the branches sway gently, but it died out before it crossed the meadows to the house, and Sugar Glider made no move to launch himself into the air.

"Err… well, everyone says he did…I mean that's why the cat went away for so long," Sam trailed off.

"Well, Sam, your grandfather certainly fought the cat, and that's a very brave thing to do. He almost got killed. And then there was no cat," said Sugar Glider. "Doesn't mean he defeated the cat."

"Mr Glider," Sam said, "My Grandfather was fond of telling stories. That is true. But he never made up a story. He was no liar."

"I never said he was Sam, and don't get upset. You came to me with questions, its not my fault if you don't like the answers," Sugar Glider said, not sounding upset in the slightest, "but I have a question for you Sam, did you grandfather ever talk about killing, or defeating the cat?"

"No," said Sam. "He never once spoke about what happened that day. It was a story he always let others tell."

They were both quiet for a time, looking out over the countryside. Sam wondered, as he often did, if out there in the forest, his Grandfather had made a little nest for himself. Sam rather fancied it was a nice warm nest looking out over the lake, and that he spent his days making friends with new and interesting creatures.

"Do you know what the secret to gliding is Sam?"

Sam just shrugged and kept looking at the forest and the lake in the distance.

"Finding the balance between lift and drag. You see, when you glide, the air flows over you. Some of that air lifts you up, takes you higher, that's lift. But some of the air holds you back, it grabs at you and slows you down, makes you drop. That's drag. The hard thing is, the more lift you get, the more drag that comes along with the lift.

"The more lift you want; the more drag you need to deal with. You have to find the balance between lift and drag. If you want to glide, you have to move through the air, you don't have any choice. But you do have a choice about how much lift you want, and how much drag you have to accept.

"And the way you control lift and drag is by attitude. Your attitude is the angle that you glide at. When you glide into the breeze you must control your attitude. If you can fly into the breeze with the correct attitude, you get lift, and the drag seems to go away. It still there, the drag, but the right attitude makes it seem to go away, and you get the best lift."

"Look Sugar Glider. I don't have time for your silly stories. I don't understand them and I don't want to," Sam said. He was very frustrated and angry.

For the first time, Sugar Glider looked hurt, and Sam regretted his words. Sugar Glider had only ever been friendly and polite to Sam.

"Sam, your grandfather was a great mouse. Great in ways you probably don't even understand, and he had courage. He knew that mice were being killed foraging for food, and that as long as it was every mouse for themselves, they would always be fighting over the food.

"It was your grandfather that saved the field mice during those lean years, when there was a hard winter, and even though the house mice didn't have much, it was your grandfather that convinced the committee to let the field mice into the house. It was your grandfather that convinced the rats that all the rodents could work together to share the food. He was a mouse of vision, but not everyone treated his vision with the respect it deserved. He watched others take his ideas and use them for their own purposes. Purposes that he didn't agree with. Some of those purposes were the opposite of what he believed in."

The breeze strengthened, and Sugar Glider stood up on his hind legs, his arms stretched out, and a beautiful membrane of fur stretched out between the tips of his arms and the tips of his feet, ruffling in the breeze.

"This wind is too good to waste Sam," Sugar Glider said with a smile.

"Lift and drag Sam. Some things have the power to lift us up, and some things have the power to drag us down. Sometimes even the things that lift us up, can drag us down. You need to make sure there is more lift than drag in your life, otherwise you won't be able to glide. That all comes down to attitude."

Sam crossed him arms and tapped his feet.

"All this talk of lift, drag, attitude. Its all well and good Sugar Glider, but I need hard information. I need to know how to fight the cat."

"The cat isn't the problem you think it is Sam. Who has said you must fight the cat? You want to stop mice being killed by the cat. Does that mean you have to fight the cat? Who says that? The committee? What about you Sam? What do you think you should do?"

"You are very annoying today Sugar Glider," Sam said. "Why can't you just speak plainly."

"Oh Sam. The committee has said you must deal with the cat. But they don't care if you deal with the cat. They just want to be seen to take action. You are that action. If you succeed, they are heroes. If you fail, they tried, but you weren't up to the task. They can't lose. But you can. The committee are not interested in mice and affiliated rodents Sam, they are interested in themselves. And protecting themselves."

"You aren't helping me. How can I defeat the CAT," Sam shouted.

"King Rat," Sugar Glider said with a sigh.

"King Rat?" said Sam 'What do you mean?'

"King Rat was there when your grandfather fought the cat. They live much longer, the rats, for all their bickering and fighting and aggression, they live longer than you mice. King Rat knew your grandfather, and King Rat was there the day your grandfather confront-ed the cat. They were friends in a weird way, your Grandfather and King Rat. I don't know why, but the strangest of people are friends. Like a sugar glider and a mouse. Fancy that."

Sugar Glider leaned into the wind, so far that it seemed like he should fall off the branch.

"See...lift, the wind is holding me here."

Sam was sad to see his friend preparing to go. He didn't want to finish the conversation still annoyed at Sugar Glider. Sugar Glider squatted down, tensed his legs.

"Go see King Rat Sam. At least you will know where you stand with the rats. But please be careful Sam... the committee isn't looking out for you."

Sugar Glider launched himself out into the air. Sam's stomach lurched, as it always did when he saw Sugar Glider leap. He could never have that much courage, to just leap out into the air, with the ground so far away.

"Remember lift and drag." Sugar Glider's voice became faint as he glided through the leaves to a nearby tree. "Find your lift Sam, and minimize your drag."

Sugar Glider was gone and Sam was all alone on a branch high in the tree.

Chapter Nine - Meet The Rats

Sam stood in the passage way that led to the laundry. Or, more accurately, down underneath the floor of the laundry. It was dark, and a little bit dank. Sam could feel warm wet air blowing up past him. It smelt moldy and there was a faint smell of *Rat* on the breeze. The smell made Sam's stomach tighten. He peered into the darkness, and fancied that he could see the glowing eyes of dozens of rats. All waiting to pounce. On him.

Gypsy and the committee had assured him that the rats and mice were friends now, and that Sam had nothing to fear from the rats.

Sam took one step forward and the shadows seemed to engulf him. He glanced back at the well lit passage behind him, leading back to the main house, and where the mice lived. It already seemed far away. He took another step. And another.

Soon he was well into the passageway under the laundry, and looking back, there was only a small slither of light showing from where he had come. Cobwebs wafted and billowed in the warm breeze, making the light seem even further away. Some of the cob webs had stuck to Sam, and he wanted to stop and pick the webs out of his fur. Instead, he kept walking slowly, trying to feel his way forward. Looking back had been a mistake, because now his eyes had to readjust to the darkness.

"Stop it Sam," he whispered to himself. "There is nothing to be scared of."

He took another step, this time a proper step, without hesitation. He fell flat on his face. From above him there was some coarse snigger's.

"Look what the cat dragged in," said a deep raspy voice. There was a chorus of chuckles. A large paw grasped onto his scruff and picked him up high, so that his feet were only just touching the ground. The smell of rat was now very strong and Sam felt his heart beating. In the gloom he saw a small alcove in the side of the corridor, and the shape of several rats standing around him.

"A little mousey where he shouldn't be," said the rat holding him up by his scruff. "What brings you here little mousey? Are you lost?"

"Err," said Sam.

It was getting a little bit hard to breathe with his skin tight around his neck. No one had held him by the scruff since he was a pup, and that was his mother. This was nothing like her gentle and caring grip. The rat gave him a violent shake, and Sam's teeth chattered together.

"What's a matter, cat got your tongue?" said the rat. The other rats all found this very funny and repeated it to each other.

"Shaddup," said the rat holding him, although the other rats kept snickering quietly.

Sam's eyes, once they stopped rolling around his head from being shaken, had started to acclimatize to the darkened corridor. He could see his captor's face now. Big rat teeth. Huge snout pushed up close to his nose. Big scars all over his face, and one ear that was almost chewed off. Still holding him up off the ground with one paw, the rat gave Sam a slap with his other paw. It wasn't a very hard slap, but it caught Sam by surprise.

"Asked you a question mousey. What'cha doen down here?"

"I, um… I've um… come to, well, King Rat that is, asked me to come to see him," Sam managed to say, trying very hard to stop his teeth chattering together. The rats all started laughing.

"King Rat? Wants to see a mouse? Well there's an unlikely story if ever I did 'ere one."

His captor lowered him down, but still kept a tight grip on Sam's scruff. He gave him another slap. Sam winced. This one was a bit harder than the last.

"Now why would King Rat want to see a little scared mousey?" the scar-faced rat said, peering down at Sam. One paw was raised and Sam braced himself for another slap.

"Well, I, err, I don't know. I was just told to come and see him."

"Told says you. Told by who I says?" Scarface gave him a little shake.

"By me," said a familiar voice from behind them.

Scar face turned, and Sam saw Roland, who didn't look as Rattish as Sam thought when he was standing with real rats.

"King Rat wants to see him Scar, and I don't think he will be too happy that you've been playing with him."

"What does King Rat want with a little mousey eh?" the scar-faced rat said.

"I don't know, and I didn't ask. You can ask King Rat yourself, but its not my place to question him. Its also not your place to question him either Scar, unless you are planning another challenge?"

Scarface scowled and lowered Sam down, letting go of his scruff. He rubbed his chewed ear.

"No, King Rat has his reasons, I'm sure, but they best be good ones I'll say. The other Rats don't like those what consort with outsiders too much."

Roland reached out and put his paw on Sam's shoulder.

"Come Sam, I'll walk with you the rest of the way."

As much as Roland made him nervous, he felt like the closest thing Sam had to a friend right now.

"I'd stay out of trouble if I were you Scar," Roland said as they walked off.

"Oh I will, I always stay away from trouble don't I. But you, my mousey friend, trouble will come looking for you. Of that I'm sure."

Sam didn't say anything, and Roland didn't respond either.

"I didn't mean for you to come down here by yourself Sam," said Roland once they were a bit further down the passageway. Some light was now filtering in from gaps in the floor boards above. "That was quite brave to come venturing down here without someone with you. The only other mouse who ever came down here by them self was your Grandfather."

"I thought...well, you didn't actually say that you were going to come and get me," Sam said. In the gloom Sam could see Roland smiling.

"No I didn't. Sorry."

They walked on in silence for a little bit.

"Would they have hurt me?" Sam asked.

'Well, they already had. I saw them slap you. But do you mean badly? No probably not. They are bullies, and enjoy having fun with those they think weaker than them, but at the moment they know that there is peace between the rats and the mice. They were just bored."

"Oh," said Sam. "That's good to know."

"Not really. Now if they see you again, they might hurt you. They won't be happy that I interfered. Scar once challenged King Rat for the title of 'King Rat' and he lost. Badly. But I think one day he fancies himself as the King of the Rats. Right now he won't challenge King Rat, which is why he let you go. But he doesn't like being told what to do by a mouse."

"But I didn't tell him what to do," Sam protested.

"No, but I did. And Scar hates me more than he hates King Rat."

"Oh, sorry I thought you meant Scar didn't like being told what to do by me, I didn't think of you as a... well, you know you."

"You didn't think I was a mouse? You think I'm a rat?" Roland said with a smile that appeared, to Sam, a little sad.

"Yes. I'm sorry, but I thought you were a rat. I thought maybe you were the rat's representative on the committee."

"I am the rat's representative on the committee. But Sam, I'm not a rat."

They emerged into a large open space, a cavern under the laundry. At the far end of the room there was a raised platform. On it stood the largest rat Sam had seen. Not that Sam had seen many rats, but this rat was large. He stood on his hind legs gnawing at a chicken drumstick. The rest of the room was filled with several dozen rats of all shapes and sizes. All sorts of sizes, but every size was bigger than Sam. Even the smallest rat was bigger than Sam, and bigger than Roland. The room's odor reeked of rat and Sam felt his legs go weak. Roland put a firm but gentle hand on his back and guided him into the room. All eyes were on them, and some of the rats were staring at Sam and they were all muttering to each other. Roland guided Sam through the room until they stood in front of the platform. Roland took a step back, leaving Sam feeling very alone.

"King Rat, this is Sam, Sam, meet King Rat."

King Rat was nibbling on the chicken drum-stick, holding it in one paw. He eyed Sam off while he gnawed on the chicken. Sam wouldn't even have been able to pick up a chicken drumstick, let alone hold it in one paw. King Rat didn't say anything for some time, just eyeing Sam as he ate. Sam could feel the rats behind him looking at him, and there was the occasional whisper.

The drumstick was only half eaten when King Rat stopped gnawing at it. With a casual flick of his wrist, he threw the drumstick into the crowd of rats. Behind him Sam could hear scuffling and snarling. He couldn't help himself. He turned and watched as several of the rats fought over the chicken bone. There were some loud squeaks and grunts from the pack of fighting rats, and Sam even saw a splash of blood. Within a minute or two most of the rats slunk off, until there was just one rat standing holding the chicken.

"They will all get some," a rough deep voice said behind. King Rat. Sam turned again.

"What?" he said before he could catch himself.

King Rat smiled, and it wasn't as scary as Sam had thought it would be.

"It's our way," continued King Rat, "even though there is enough food, we like the sport of it. The winner will have first pick, and will then distribute the food to the other rats. We respect a rat that can stick up for himself. Anyway, we've been formally introduced, but not informally."

King Rat stuck out his paw. Sam stared at it for a moment, before realizing that King Rat wanted him to shake it.

"Oh," said Sam and stuck out his paw and they shook hands. "Thank you your highness for helping me with the cat."

King Rat chuckled.

"King Rat. My title is King Rat. No need to call me 'your highness'. And you are most welcome. Very brave of you to jump on to a cat's tail, I must say. I haven't ever seen a mouse do something as brave. Not even your grandfather would have done that. Now, lets go talk in private."

Without another word, King Rat turned and walked off through a small door in the side of the room. Sam guessed he should follow. He turned and looked at Roland, who just nodded at him. Sam followed King Rat through the door. Behind him all Sam could hear was rats fighting over scraps.

The sounds of the bickering rats faded as Sam followed King Rat down a short tunnel. A gentle breeze flowed down the tunnel, smelling fresh and dry, unlike the dank, wet atmosphere in King Rat's hall.

King Rat pushed open a door, and motioned for Sam to step through it.

To Sam's surprise, the door opened out into a spacious, well lit room. It was very neat and tidy, not at all what Sam would have expected from a rat. All of the furniture was quite large by mouse standards, but it was still very nice, and Sam would have felt quite at home, if the furniture was the right size.

"My home. Or rather the home of the king of the rats. Which is me. For now."

"It's very nice," said Sam, not sure what else he should say.

"Not what you expected from a rat eh? Did you think we live in nests made from shredded newspaper and mouse bones?" King Rat smiled at Sam, and Sam smiled back. He thought King Rat was joking, but he wasn't sure.

"I've got something I'd like you to see Sam," said King Rat, motioning Sam through another door.

Inside the next room there was a large comfortable arm chair, with a table. On that table was a beautiful hand carved chess set. There was a game in progress on the board. It wasn't obvious which side was winning. On the other side of the table was a small chair on very long legs. Not unlike a high chair that you might put a pup in when teaching it table manners.

"Take a seat." King Rat said and gestured to the high chair.

"Oh, I don't play very well at all," said Sam looking at the game in progress.

"No one around here does. Well, not anymore at least. I don't think we should play a game. I think we should talk. Take a seat, I won't be a moment."

King Rat went back into the other room and Sam could hear him bustling about. Sam climbed up into the high set chair. It was very comfortable. The chair had a good view of the table, but more impressively, a window was set next to it. The window was cut into the side of the laundry wall at ground level. Sam looked out and saw that King Rats home overlooked the back lawn. He could see the whole yard. He looked out across the finely cut lawn, and across to the far side of the yard, where there was a small concrete border, and then beyond that longer grass, and in the distance he could see the start of the forest. Looking up he saw the huge oak tree where he often met with Sugar Glider. In fact, if he craned his head slightly he could see the very branch that he and Sugar Glider had sat on when they talked. From here it looked very high up. He looked around to see if he could see sugar glider, but there was no sign of him.

"He's not there at the moment," King Rat said, as he came back into the room with a big tray. He set the tray down, and Sam saw a simple but tasty array of cheeses and fruit. There was a mug of coffee, and fine china pot and a single china cup.

"I see you two, up there, talking. I don't know the sugar glider really, but I'm told they are very friendly creatures. It makes me smile. You are very different from your grandfather, but you have some things in common. Your grandfather always spoke very highly of the sugar gliders."

"Did you know my grandfather very well?" Sam asked.

King Rat sat down opposite Sam, but didn't say anything. He appeared deep in thought as he poured Sam tea from the pot. He put the coffee down in front of himself, and motioned for Sam to help himself to the cheese. Being a polite mouse, Sam waited for his host to start. The tea smelt very nice. Far more delicate than he would have expected to be served in a rat's den.

"We played chess a lot. Your grandfather and I. He was both a very easy mouse to know, and in some ways a very hard mouse to know. He talked a lot. He told a lot of stories. He taught me a lot with those stories."

"Do you know how he defeated the cat?" Sam asked.

King Rat frowned. "I thought you wanted to know about your grandfather. That's just one thing in his life. Its not the thing that defines him. Your grandfather was more than that one thing," King Rat said, taking a sip of his coffee and staring down at the chess board.

"I know, its just...well I want to know more about him, but this whole cat thing seems to be the most important thing for me to know. I need to know how he did it," Sam said.

King Rat just kept staring at the chess board.

"You did it didn't you? You fought and defeated the cat. Just like you helped me? My grandfather didn't defeat the cat at all."

King Rat picked up one of the chess pieces and examined it. It was a pawn, carved in the shape of a field mouse on all four paws.

"Do you know this game was the last game I played with your grandfather. I haven't actually played a game in this room since he left. We were half way through the game when word came to us that there was a pup and his parents trapped by the cat. We didn't know at the time that it was you and your parents. After your parents died, I think he got caught up in things, and we never finished the game. I miss playing chess here. I especially miss playing chess with him.

"You must understand something about rats Sam, even though we live in packs, we are very much individuals. Rats believe that everyone must make his or her own way in life. We respect strength and cunning. We admire rats who will do what it takes to survive. A rat that tries to help others without any selfish reason is seen as weak. The other rats won't respect you unless they fear you a little bit."

"Did you defeat the cat?" Sam asked.

"No Sam. I did not defeat the cat. Your grandfather didn't defeat the cat. We fought with the cat. Your grandfather managed to lure the cat into the living room. It was incredibly brave, although, perhaps not as brave as jumping onto a cat's tail. While your grandfather distracted the cat, I jumped on and bit his ear. Took a nice little piece out of it too." King Rat smiled at Sam. "We didn't really plan it, but we had spoken before of how we might stand up to the cat. I always told him it was a silly idea. Like I say, we rats don't do things to help others out."

"But," Sam said, "you helped him. You helped me. We could do it again."

"Sam, your grandfather taught me to see differently. He showed me that you can be strong and proud, but that didn't mean you had to be cruel. I still believe that everyone has to stand on their own hind legs. But I'll tell you again. We didn't defeat the cat. We fought it, and gave a good account of ourselves, but we almost got eaten, and the cat was very angry. We probably would have lost many more mice and rats if we weren't lucky."

"Lucky?" Sam said.

"Well, maybe not lucky. Your grandfather used to say 'Luck is what happens when preparation meets opportunity'"

King Rat put the pawn down and picked up another piece, it was the queen, carved in the shape of a field mouse, but unlike the pawns, the queen was standing on her hind legs with a strong noble look on her face. Sam thought it quite odd to have a field mouse as the queen.

"You must see the bigger picture Sam. This house we live in. Its not ours. We creep around in the corridors, we 'forage' for food. It may be our home, but its not our house.

"Even the cat doesn't have the right to call the house 'his'. The humans. Its theirs. We live by their grace, or indifference. You can either accept that, or not. They come for a period of time. And they go. Where, I don't know, but when they are here, the cat is here. When they go. The cat goes. It just so happened that after we fought the cat, the humans left the house for a time. Now they are back, and so is the cat.

"So what do we do now?" Sam asked. "How can we make them leave, or at least make the cat leave?"

"Freedom and happiness are won by disregarding things that lie beyond our control. You cannot control the cat. You cannot control the humans. Until you understand that you cannot be happy, nor free. Its only when you accept it that you will be happy and free."

Sam wasn't sure what to make of this, and so said nothing. King Rat was silent for a few minutes.

"Your grandfather and I spoke often about how we might deal with the cat. I always said it was a foolish notion, but your grandfather believed that with teamwork and a bit of cunning we could do it. I told him that we should just stockpile food when the cat wasn't here and then wait it out when the cat was here. We argued about it a lot.

"When you and your parents got trapped, he didn't wait for any help. He just went straight in and tried to fight the cat. I heard about it and ran to the living room as fast as I could, hoping that your grandfather would remember some of the plans we had talked about. I don't know if it was luck or if he managed it, but he lured the cat into living room. I bit the cat, which allowed your grandfather to run back into the kitchen to rescue you. I left at that stage, I was a bit angry with your grandfather for not calling me to help. It was only later that I heard that his son, your father had been killed by the cat.

"You know what I love about chess Sam? It was the time I spent learning from your grandfather. But here is what I've learnt since, by looking at the board after he and I stopped playing. You can craft these beautiful pieces, like I did. I carved them myself. And you can lay out the board, with all the pieces on them. And you can play a game. But each piece has to play the game according to what the rules say that piece can do. There is nothing the player can do, except play each piece according to its strengths and weaknesses.

"Look at the Queen. She doesn't rule. The King does. But she is the most powerful piece on the board. She can do almost anything. She is so powerful that some players never use her, they are too scared to risk her."

King Rat put the queen down, back where it had come from and picked up the pawn again.

"Look at this pawn. Its the weakest piece. The poor field mouse. There are so many of them. Most players treat them casually. Throw them away. Sometimes they even get in the way and players deliberately sacrifice them to clear the board. But what happens if the poor pawn makes it across to the far side of the board?"

"It becomes a queen?" said Sam.

"No. The player actually chooses what it becomes. It can become any other piece on the board. But players normally choose the queen."

King Rat put the pawn down and picked up another piece. This one was the black King, it was the shape of large rat standing on its hind legs. He examined it in detail, as if looking at it for the first time.

"Interesting piece the King. Its the most important piece on the board, but it has the least power," King Rat said. "All the other pieces defend the king, or attack the other king. The king himself appears impressive, but in reality has very little power. The King only has power because we agree that the King has power. Because all the other pieces *behave* as if the King has power."

"The point I am making Sam, is that everything we understand about the world around us is not real, its a fiction, one that we all made up together."

"Of course its real." Sam interrupted. "If the cat kills a mouse, the mouse is dead. That's real."

"Yes," said King Rat, "the things that happen around us are real. But how we understand those things, that's not real. Its something we made up. The committee, the power it has. Its not real. You let them have power. So the power is real because you let it be real. You can take that power away by not believing in it. This queen. When she is on the board, she has to follow the rules. Take her off the board, then she isn't a chess piece any more. But that makes her free. She is powerful on the board, but only within the rules.

King Rat was silent for a long while. Sam sat still, looking at the chess board as if it would help him make sense of what King Rat was saying.

"It wasn't until a while after that fight that I learnt that the cat, before your grandfather managed to rescue you, had already killed your father and mother. Attacking the cat only gave your grandfather time to rescue you. Your grandfather never spoke about attacking the cat again after that day."

"So, Sam, you see, I feel like in some way, I've had a part to play in your life."

"Sam," King Rat continued. "When I heard that the *committee* had nominated you to deal with the cat, I thought that you deserved to know the truth about that day." King Rat said committee like it was a curse.

"You don't like the committee?" Sam asked.

"No. I don't trust them. Mice and Affiliated Rodents. Hmmph. At least with rats you know where you stand. A rat will always look after himself first, and respects strength and cunning. The committee. Bunch of self serving politicians. I don't trust them as far as I can throw them."

"But the rats are part of the committee aren't they? Affiliated Rodents?" Sam asked.

"No. There are no 'affiliated rodents' on the committee. That's just a title they gave themselves to convince the mice that they had support from other rodents. The rats have an observer on the committee. I've named Roland as my official observer. He doesn't scare them as much as a rat would."

"But, Roland told me he isn't a rat. " Sam said.

"His mother was a field mouse and his father was a rat. It is said to be impossible, a rat and a mouse. But his father loved his mother very very much, and maybe that was enough. The mice think him a rat, and the rats think him a mouse. Its a hard life for him."

"So he's not a rat or a mouse?" Sam asked.

"He is what he thinks he is."

"That makes no sense. He's either a rat or a mouse or something else."

"What makes you what you are? You are a mouse. You are a mouse because you have the body of a mouse, and the mind of a mouse. You cannot do much about your body. But your mind is yours to control. Most animals let their minds control them. They sit back and accept the way things are and let their mind chatter away without any control.

"But a wise animal learns to control their mind. To make their mind do as they tell it. If a mouse wanted to be a rat, he could eat more, exercise more, become bigger, but he would not be a rat, he'd just be a big strong mouse. And he would wait and think 'when I am this big, or this strong, then I will be a rat'. But he will never be a rat until he decides in his mind to be a rat, and he makes his mind think like a rat.

"Roland is what Roland thinks himself to be. I don't know what that is, and its not important. Roland is happy with who he is, because he has decided what he is." King Rat said

"What do you want to be Sam?"

"A writer," Sam said softly.

"And you never will be Sam." King Rat said. "Not until you stop wanting to be a writer start being a writer. Don't think about what it will take to 'be' a writer. You must actually be a writer, and then think about how you would be better writer. Act like a writer, think like a writer, do what a writer does. Don't try to be a writer. Be a writer. Do what a writer does. Write.

"I'm tired Sam, I'm not the rat I once was, and soon some young rat will challenge me for the title. That makes me sad. Not because I will die, but because I still haven't finished what I wanted to accomplish. Your grandfather opened my eyes to a lot of things. We rats have our good side and our bad side. I set out to bring out the good side, independent, strong, cunning. But I think once I go, the bad side of the rats will come back out. Selfish, cruel and coarse."

King Rat sat back. He looked very tired. Sam didn't really know what to say. He knew very little about rats.

"It was your grandfather's fate as well. He saw the best in mice. It was your grandfather that brought the field mice in to the house when they were starving. He taught the field mice to forage in the house, he showed the committee that they could stockpile food to get them through the tough times. He had a vision for a community of mice, not field mice, not house mice, just mice. But he watched as the house mice forced the field mice to forage, while the house mice just sat back and didn't take any risks.

"I think after your parents died, he lost heart. He saw that the committee weren't interested in making things better for all mice, just for themselves."

"What should I do then?" Sam asked. "The cat still needs to be dealt with. Mice are still dying."

"There will always be cats. And if not cats, something else. Who said its your job to deal with it? The committee...but who are they to tell you what you should do. Do what you think you should do. Do what you think is right."

#

Sam ducked under a cobweb hanging from a pipe as he and Roland walked out of the rat's lair.

"He's not well Sam. He hides it very well, but he's getting older, and I think he is losing interest," Roland said.

Sam hadn't seen any of the other rats as they left. King Rat had grown tired at the end of their conversation and called for Roland to take Sam back home.

"Why doesn't he step down. Let another rat become King?"

Roland laughed.

"You don't step down from being King Rat. Another rat challenges you, and you fight. The loser dies, or is sent away into exile," Roland said.

"Why doesn't he do that. Not the fight to the death bit, but go away? Would it be so bad?" Sam asked.

"I think he is still a rat at heart. He still wants to rule the rats, and he still hopes he can improve their life. Better than someone like Scar would anyway. And then there is me."

"You?"

"Yes. He worries that when he is gone, that the Rats will turn on me, and the mice would have no use for me. A father's love for his son."

Sam stopped mid-step and looked at Roland in surprise.

"Father?"

"Yes. Didn't you know? King Rat is my father."

Chapter Ten - Waiting It Out

"That's your plan? That's YOUR PLAN?"

"Well, its not a plan as such, its really...well, a strategy so to speak," Sam said, rather wishing he hadn't told Gypsy before he had thought his ideas through. But she had dropped by with some cake for afternoon tea and Sam thought she would be able to help him turn his idea into a plan. But it wasn't working out quite the way Sam thought it would.

"That's not a plan. That's a stupid idea. Wait it out. Wait it out. What kind of an idiot says 'Wait it out'? Do you think the committee needed Sam Mouse to tell them 'wait it out'?"

Sam looked at the ground. He wasn't sure what to say.

"Well? Well?" Gypsy demanded.

"Well, King Rat says that..."

"King Rat. King Rat," Gypsy shrieked at him. "You think King Rat cares about the mice? He is struggling to even stay in charge of the rats."

"But he says that…"

"I don't care what a *rat* says. I care what mice are saying. You are embarrassing me. Just today someone said, 'What's your Sam doing about the cat?' My Sam? MY SAM? Do you know how embarrassed I felt? What should I say? Sam is doing nothing? Sam is a dreamer? Sam is scared?"

"I'm not scared Gypsy...well, I am a bit scared, but its not that. I don't think fighting the cat will do anything. We need to find another way."

"You, Sam, think you are smarter than the committee. But you are not. If you were, you would be ON the committee. But you are not. You, SAM, need to do what the committee has told you to do. Deal. With. The. Cat."

Gypsy glared at him. Sam felt shock. Last night he had imagined how this conversation would go, but it had turned out nothing like he had expected. Although now that he thought about it, his idea of waiting for the cat to go away was rather silly. There wasn't any action at all in that action plan.

To Sam's relief, there was a knock at the door. Gypsy went quiet, but she was glaring at Sam, who opened the door. Damon the dapper mouse stood there smiling.

"Not interrupting anything am I Sam old boy? Oh, hello there Gypsy. Looking lovely as ever. A tad annoyed though. You'll get frown lines if you keep glaring like that," Damon gave Sam a little nudge with his elbow as he walked in. Gypsy switched her glare from Sam to Damon.

"Never mind Gypsy, Sam. She's got a very hot temper, never happy if the world isn't giving her what she deserves. Or what she thinks she deserves," Damon smiled at Gypsy. Gypsy stomped her foot once and then pushed past Sam and Damon and stormed out of Sam's apartment.

"Anyway Sam Old Boy. Thought you should know. A very good opportunity presents itself. Well an opportunity for someone, either you or the cat. Depending on which way one looks at it. The cat is in the kitchen, and the committee thinks now would be a perfect opportunity for you to further the good work you started. Strike while the cats on the back paw, so to speak. So come on Sam, for I think its time you went down to the kitchen and put your plans into action."

Sam still didn't have a plan. Other than wait. But it didn't seem like it was a plan that involved action.

"Come on old boy, there is quite an audience gathering now that the committee has passed word that you are going to face down the cat. Don't want to disappoint your fans do you?"

Chapter Eleven - Mr Montagu's Plan

Sam stood in the mouse hole that led to the kitchen. Mr Montagu and Damon stood next to him. He could see the passageway lined with mice, all looking through gaps in the skirting board. Gypsy stood next to Mr Montagu. She still seemed annoyed at him. She was smiling, but Sam thought her eyes seemed hard and sharp.

"So, Mr Montagu, I can't really see the cat," Sam said, peering through the hole, looking around the kitchen floor.

"Oh, he's there all right. Foraging party saw him. He's up on the table. What we'll do is send one of the foraging party over to the pantry."

Mr Montagu clapped a rather young and scruffy looking field mouse on the back. The field mouse didn't look too happy to be there.

"The cat will pounce on him...err...well, try to pounce eh? Young Max here is fast, so the cat won't...shouldn't get him. That's your cue Sam. A repeat of your last encounter. You run out there while the cat's back is turned and run up his tail. This time however don't stop at his tail. Run all the way up his mangy old back and give him a good old bite on the ear. Keep nipping him. Try not to let go, might not work out so well for you if you do.

"Then, this pack of field mice here will run out and grab his tail, just like you did." Mr Montague pointed to a bunch of even smaller and more nervous field mice. "Look at them Sam, inspired by your courage, they'll give that cat a beating he'll never forget. Then that beast will stay away from mice in future."

Sam thought the field mice looked scared rather than inspired.

"That's the plan?" Sam asked.

"Why, yes Sam. That is the plan. Have you any better?"

Gypsy leaned forward and said, "You can do it Sam. We all believe in you." she leaned forward to give him a hug and whispered in his ear. "*If you don't go out there, everyone will know you are a coward.*" She leaned back and said, "Your grandfather would be so proud of you right now."

"Right oh Max," said Mr Montagu to the young field mouse who was to run across the kitchen floor. "Off you go. We're all watching. Do us proud." Mr Montagu gave the nervous field mouse a solid push out into the open.

Max stood out there on the edge of the kitchen floor, looking around. Mr Montagu thumped the wall, and several of the other mice in the wall did the same. Sam heard movement up on the table, then he saw a tuft of orange fur swaying back and forth across the top of the table, and then a large head with green eyes peered over the edge, fixing Max in its awful gaze.

Max looked back at the hole. Past Mr Montague to Sam.

"Mr Sam?" he said.

"Don't look at us," Mr Montagu roared. "Do your job. RUN."

Max ran.

Max ran faster than Sam had seen any mouse run. He moved so fast that Sam felt like time was slowing down. Max was half way across the floor before the cat even blinked an eye. But when Max was halfway across the room, without any warning, the cat launched itself in a single smooth leap and landed on all fours right in the centre of the room. In front of Max. Right between Max and the pantry. Max froze. He was meant to run *to* the pantry, but now that the cat stood between him and the pantry, there was nowhere for him to go, except back.

Sam had been steeling himself for a sprint across the kitchen floor while the cat was turned away from him. But now the cat was looking back towards the mouse hole.

Max was staring at the cat. Mesmerized by the cats twitching tail and menacing grin. He glanced back towards the safety of the hole and slowly started to step back towards the hole, so far away.

"What are you going to do now? Cat didn't jump where it was supposed to," Mr Montagu said. "Looks like your plan has a few flaws in it."

My plan? Sam thought. *This was NEVER my plan!*

Max took another step closer to the hole. In the blink of an eye the cat launched itself into the air, spinning around and landing on the other side of Max. Now the cat was between Max and the safety of the hole. But its back was now to Sam.

All Sam could see was the cats body, hunched over, and its paws moving back and forth. In the passageway behind Sam some of the field mice started to cry out. From further up the passageway a mouse shouted, "He's OK. The cats just playing with him."

He is NOT Ok. Thought Sam, for now he could see that the cat was softly batting at Max with its paws, but its claws were not out. *Its only a matter of time before the cat gets bored and kills him.*

Someone tried to push past Sam. It was Michelle. She was sobbing as she pushed past Sam and Mr Montagu and into the kitchen. Sam looked. The cat still had its back to the hole. Sam braced himself.

This is still not a very good plan, thought Sam

He ran out onto the floor. As fast as he could go. Straight up onto the cats back and before he knew it, he was standing on the cats head. One paw holding on to each ear. The cat sat bolt upright in surprise.

"Run. Run. Run," Sam yelled out to Max.

Max hesitated. He seemed to want to run back to the safety of the hole, but he also looked a few times at the pantry. After a second, he kept running for the pantry. The cat still seemed in shock. It tensed itself up to go after Max, seeming to forget there was a mouse on its head.

Sam looked over his shoulder and looked at the cat's tail. Suddenly he wished he was holding on to the tail rather than standing on the cat's head. Even though the tail could whip around fast, it felt safer than standing exposed on the cat's head. Sam braced himself. He took a deep breath. *This is still a really silly plan* he thought. With a loud yell in the cat's ears, he pulled hard on each ear, alternating between the left ear and the right ear. The cat hissed and stood with all four legs straight, its back arched. Sam could see the cat's claws extending and retracting. The hissing became a hideous yowling. Sam had never heard such a loud sound before. He gave the ears another hard tweak.

Sam glanced back at the mouse hole. Michelle was standing just at the entrance. Further back in the hole he could just make out Mr Montagu. He stuck his head far enough forward to yell something and wave his arm towards the lounge room. Sam couldn't hear what he was saying over the terrible yodeling of the cat, but he guessed Mr Montagu was telling him to get the cat into the lounge room.

He gave the left ear a strong tug to see if the cat would turn to the left. Instead the cats right paw came rushing up, sweeping across the top of its head, claws fully extended. Sam managed to duck down low and the paw swept past him, but Sam wasn't confident that the next swipe would miss.

From the hole Sam saw the team of mice streaming out, but they were headed across to the pantry, not coming out to help him. The cat gave another swipe, this time from the other direction. Sam's heart sank. Sam let go of the cat's ears and tried to run down the cat's back. He got as far as the cat's front shoulders when the cat started to spin around. Sam lay flat on the cats back, all four paws spread out, holding onto tufts of cat hair. *If only the cat would stop spinning!* Sam thought.

Suddenly, the cat stopped spinning.

The cat rolled. It rolled in one quick motion. So quick, that Sam had not even let go of the cat's hair. The cat rolled right over and back onto its feet. Sam was almost crushed under the weight of the cat, and it was only the speed with which the cat rolled that saved him. Sam felt the cat tensing up, ready for another roll

This time the cat rolled with its shoulders against the floor, and Sam was trapped beneath the cat. Sam could hardly breathe, his mouth was stuffed full of cat's hair, and he could see stars in front of his eyes. As suddenly as the cat had rolled onto him, the cat rolled off. Sam lay on the floor gathering his breath. The world seemed to be blurry and everything was spinning around him. He took a deep breath. And another, and the world stopped spinning, and things came into focus.

Sam lay there on his back, looking up at the ceiling of the kitchen. It seemed very close. It seemed to be moving, and then he realized that he was laying underneath the cat, looking at the cats belly. Sam managed to stand up, even though the floor still seemed to be swaying underneath him. Across the kitchen floor he could see Michelle helping Max back towards the safety of the hole in the skirting board. Sam could also see some of the field mice also running across the floor, hunks of bread on their backs.

The cat seemed to have forgotten him, distract-ed by the mice running back from the pantry. Sam only just managed to roll out of the way as the cat crouched down on all fours, readying itself to pounce on one of the bread laden field mice.

Sam sighed. *I need to come up with a better plan!*. He ran around to the cat's tail, took a deep breath and bit down hard. The cat leapt up onto the table, and Sam, still holding onto the tail with his paws and teeth, was dragged up with the cat. Sam dangled over the edge of the table, hanging from the end of the tail. He closed his eyes took a deep breath and then let go, landing on all four paws as he hit the floor. Some of the field mice running back from the pantry stopped to help him.

Mr Montagu stepped out of the hole, yelling. "The food! Get the food! Don't worry about Sam, he can look after himself." The yelling caught the cat's attention and he looked sharply at where Mr Montagu was standing. Mr Montagu ran back into the hole and was quiet.

Sam managed to catch his breath. The cat stared at him from the top of the table, and then back at its tail, then at Sam. Finally, it crouched down and jumped onto the chair, bracing itself to jump again. Sam didn't wait around to see what it did next, despite feeling like his whole body had been jammed in a vice, he ran towards the hole.

All of the other mice had made it to the safety of the hole. Mice were packed around the inside of the passageway, so tightly that Sam could only just get inside the hole. Behind him he could feel air rushing past him as the cat's paw swiped down across the hole. Sam felt a small prick on his back and pushed a bit further in to the passageway. He turned around and saw the cat's paw, pushed as far as it could go into the hole, needle sharp claws extended, only just reaching where Sam had been standing. "Move," Sam shouted, while trying to gulp in another breath.

The mice all scurried further into the passageway.

The cat's paw withdrew, to be replaced by one big cats eye. The mice all moved even further away from the entrance, and the cat settled back a few feet, laying down, staring into the hole.

In the passageway behind the skirting boards, Sam could hear Mr Montagu talking to the field mice that had foraged in the pantry. "Look here. This is a very shabby haul indeed. All you've managed to get is stale bread and dry biscuits. Where is the cheese? Where is the cake? Not even fresh bread. Poor Old Sam was out there risking his life while you miserable chaps couldn't even be bothered getting decent food."

Mr Montagu looked up and saw Sam standing in the passageway.

"Look here is Sam Mouse now," he said "He does look quite angry. You chaps should hang your heads in shame."

Some of the field mice did indeed look down at the floor. One or two of them glanced at Sam before hanging their heads. Sam was indeed angry. He couldn't recall ever feeling this angry before.

"What happened to your plan Montagu?" he cried out. "You said the field mice were going to help me with the cat. Why did they go foraging? I could have been killed out there, and for what? Some hunks of bread?"

"Now look here Sam old boy. Plans change. I saw an opportunity, and I took it. That's why I'm on the committee, I see opportunities that you don't. You were dealing with the cat just fine, so I thought we'd take the opportunity to forage some more. Didn't think you'd let go and run so quickly. You should have kept that beast distracted a bit longer."

"Run? Run?" Sam cried. "I didn't RUN, I was squashed, and then dropped from a great height."

"Settle down. Settle down. Next time, you'll need to lift your game a little bit, a bit more courage is what you need Sam. Now, I suggest you go home, you're a bit over wrought. I've got some committee business to attend to." Mr Montagu turned his attention back to the field mice. "Take this rubbish that you collected down to the food store. No point wasting it, even if it is stale." He walked off down the passage-way.

The field mice started gathering up the food that they had collected. Sam looked around and saw that Michelle and one of the other field mice was helping Max to stand up.

"He is Ok," she said. "Just a small scratch and a bit of shock."

"Thank you," Sam said. "It was very brave of you to run out like that to rescue him, but you shouldn't have taken such a big risk."

Michelle shrugged. "I couldn't let you face the cat like that alone, after everything you've done for us."

But Sam couldn't really think of anything that he had actually done for the field mice. After all, the cat was still on the loose.

"You were hurt Sam," Michelle said. "Do you need Max and I to help you home?"

Sam looked at Max who had suffered worse than Sam had at the hands of the cat. His hair was matted with cat saliva, and he had several small cuts on his body.

"No," said Sam "You need to look after Max and the other mice. I will be fine."

Chapter Twelve - The Field Mice

Sam woke to a loud knocking on the door. He moaned and tucked his head under his paws and tried to snuggle down deeper into his nest. Even though he had slept after his dream (or nightmare.), he felt very tired and would happily have stayed in bed for the rest of the day.

The knocking continued.

"Go away," yelled Sam.

"Well at least I know you are in there," came Roland's muffled voice through the door. "Come on Sam, I've got something to show you. I'll get you breakfast. My treat."

Sam groaned, but he knew Roland wouldn't go away, so he got up and opened the door.

"What do you want?" he said.

"Oh, and they say rats are rude," said Roland, smiling.

"Well, you keep stopping me from sleeping," Sam said.

"Time enough to sleep when you're dead. I've got things to show you, things you should see. And its a nice day outside. Come on Sam my friend. Let's go, I'll get you some breakfast when we are out."

#

Roland and Sam stood watching the sun rise over the back yard. The sun rise was beautiful, and it was very peaceful standing on the back step watching the sky turn from deep red, to orange, to full light. Sam had never really sat and watched a sunrise. Not in total silence. It was very relaxing.

A light breeze ruffled Roland's hair, and Sam shivered. It was still cool in the morning breeze. Roland was silhouetted by the rising morning sun. Roland looked quite noble, standing on the back porch surveying the yard, and the fields beyond.

"I like to come here and watch the sunrise sometimes, it gives me a moment to think about things," said Roland.

Sam started to feel a bit nervous. He'd never been outside other than on his visits to Sugar Glider. He glanced up into the sky looking for hawks, or eagles or even an owl. Roland however didn't seem worried.

"What things?" Sam asked.

"The things I have to be grateful for. I think about how little time there is in life, and how it would be easy to waste it wishing things could be different. I think about the mean or hurtful things said about me and realize that I do not need to worry about those things, other than to make sure I do not say mean or hurtful things."

Sam wondered what mean things anyone could say that would be hurtful to a rat. But then Roland wasn't a rat.

"No one likes me Sam," Roland said. As if he were saying that it was a nice day.

"I know," said Sam, before he could stop himself. He felt very rude, for even though Roland made him nervous, Sam hated the idea of being rude. "I'm sorry" he said "What I mean is..."

"Its all right." Roland interrupted. "I know there are reasons why no one likes me. The Rats don't like me because I'm not really a rat, and they see me as a weakness on my father's behalf. The mice don't like me because I look like a rat." Roland made an exaggerated gnashing action, his teeth flashing in the morning sun. Sam laughed and suddenly Roland didn't make him feel as nervous.

"But it's OK Sam, I've learnt one thing in all my thinking. Life is empty and meaningless."

"That's very sad," Sam said.

"Not at all, in fact it makes me very content. For if life is empty, then I can choose how I fill it. An empty life can be filled with anything I want. If life has no meaning, then the very meaning of life is up to me to choose. When other people tell you what life's meaning is, they are forcing their meaning on you. Don't let them do that."

This all sounded very confusing to Sam, particularly coming from a rat. Sam expected rats to use coarse words. Grunts and curses. But then Roland wasn't a proper rat. Roland was silent again for a few moments, then with a shake of his head and a sweep of his paw, Roland indicated out beyond the yard

"Do you know what lies out there?" he asked.

"Out...there?" Sam asked.

"Where?"

"In the forest. You should go there one day. Its beautiful. Go there and you will see. I think you will find some answers to your questions in the forest."

"Questions? The only question I have is what to do about his cat," Sam said.

"The cat may be the most urgent question for you, but it is not the most important question," Roland said. "The unexamined life is a wasted one Sam. You are full of questions; you are just not asking them."

"Everyone is telling me what to do. Where to go. I'm tired of it. The committee says I have to defeat the cat. You say I have to go into the forest. Why? Nobody has any clear reasons for telling me to do anything. What will I find in that forest Roland? What? Will I find a way to fight the cat without being killed myself?"

Roland smiled at him. Despite Sam's anger, Roland appeared very relaxed. "I don't know what you will find. I know I found answers to questions out there. But my questions were probably different to yours. But I do know that you won't find any answers with the committee. You won't find any answers in all your papers and writings. You need to take action Sam, but that doesn't mean doing what the committee wants of you."

"The thing is Sam. You have to ask yourself what is important to you. I think you don't know what is important to you, that's the problem," Roland replied.

"Mice will continue to die. They will continue to die no matter what you do. The committee has made that your responsibility now. But is it your responsibility Sam? The committee doesn't want a solution; it wants an appearance of a solution. They don't care about you Sam, and they don't care about the field mice. If you wish to fight the cat, then just one more mouse will die. But if you want to stop mice dying, then killing the cat may not be the answer."

Sam stamped his hind foot. "Must everyone speak in riddles? Why won't you say what you mean? I'm a simple house mouse, I don't know what you mean."

Roland smiled, and whilst he probably meant well, Sam still thought it a little bit menacing.

"Well, Sam. You are indeed a house mouse, and a house is where a house mouse is most comfortable. But what separates the house mice from the field mice?"

"Oh...well," Sam paused, because everything that came into his mind about the difference between field mice and house mice was, well, wrong. They weren't smelly. They were actually very polite, and hard working. In fact, most field mice, now that Sam had met some of them, seemed harder working than the house mice that Sam knew.

"I don't know. Actually...there is no difference really. We just call them field mice. And we call ourselves house mice."

"No," Roland said. "Well, yes, but no. Yes, there is no difference. You are all mice. But there is a difference. The field mice came from the fields. They only came in to the house because your grandfather and the committee told them that life would be better here, that there was regular food available.

"But the truth is, the field mice could be just as happy out in the fields. There are too many of us here Sam. The cat comes and goes, but sooner or later the humans will notice how much food we steal. Between the mice and the rats, we are taking a lot of food. They won't like it. We survive because we haven't been noticed by the humans. But when they do notice, they will do something. Smoke us out with poison. Plug our holes with glue. Then more than one mouse or rat will die. The committee can't, or won't, see this. Even if they could, they can't change their thoughts. They have no vision and they are stuck because they value their possessions and their things. Their nick-knacks are more important to them than the truth. And the truth is we live here by the good grace or ignorance of other's."

Roland stopped and stared out over the fields.

"Your grandfather had vision, but the committee stole it and turned it into something else. King Rat has vision, but he is too old and the rats are too independent to change their ways."

Sam still felt very exposed standing on the back step, but the longer he stood there the more confident he felt. He looked, and high up above he could actually see Sugar Glider scampering along a branch, no doubt climbing higher to catch a morning breeze. He waved to Sugar Glider, although he knew that Sugar Glider probably couldn't see him. It made him feel good knowing Sugar Glider was up there. From the steps Sam could also see the laundry, off to the side. He looked down at ground level and saw the little crack in the wall that was the window into King Rat's lair. He couldn't make out King Rat, but he rather fancied he saw the chess set, laid out, waiting for someone to finish the old game.

"But there was a reason the field mice came in. A terrible famine. That's why they came to the house. There is food and shelter here, in the fields...what is there? Nothing," Sam said.

Roland looked down at Sam with a sideways smile.

"There are places beyond the fields, places warm and safe...in the forest. Its rather nice, and I think that a wise mouse could teach the field mice to stockpile food and to build their nests in safer spots than in the field. The journey is long, at least it is for a mouse. I have done it several times, looking for your grandfather."

This surprised Sam. He hadn't thought of Roland as an explorer.

"Why were you looking for my grandfather?" Sam asked.

"He was a great mouse. King Rat respected him greatly. I've never felt like I fit in here. I've played a role, between the rats and the mice. But neither care for me. I had this silly idea that your grandfather would understand. I also know that your grandfather never planned on things turning out this way. I think he really planned on helping the field mice find a better home. He never planned that the committee would treat the field mice so badly. Also, King Rat really wants to finish that chess game. I think he was about to beat your grandfather for the first time."

"Have you told the field mice any of this?" Sam asked.

"Not yet. No. I think they are ready to hear it, but not from me. They trust me, because of my mother, but they fear me because of my father. They are ready, but they need a leader Sam."

"Michelle?" Sam asked.

"She is a leader. There is no doubt that the field mice look up to her. If she says go, they will go. Or at least listen seriously. But she needs help Sam. She feels responsible for the orphans. It would be hard for her to make such a bold decision, knowing that she has so much responsibility for others. It weighs heavily on her, and she needs someone else to trust. All the other field mice that were leaders are gone. That's what is so evil about the committee forcing them to forage. The true leaders, the bold ones go foraging when its most dangerous. And are killed first."

Sam looked up in the trees. He could see Sugar Glider running along a branch, his tail, normally filled with a bouncing life of its own, was instead, straight. Sugar Glider was running fast for a hollow in the tree trunk.

"Hawks," Roland hissed. "See, beyond the trees."

Sam looked up and saw the beautiful but scary symmetry of a hawk wheeling above them. It hadn't seen them yet, but it would soon. Roland pushed Sam back under the door step, and followed behind him.

"And you want the field mice to go live out there? Where a hawk could get them in the open?" Sam asked.

Roland laughed. "Well, at least they will know who their enemies are. In the house they think they are protected, when they aren't. Out there, they will learn to look after themselves and stand on their own four paws. The illusion of safety is worse than the reality of danger."

#

"Keep up Sam," Roland called out behind him as they scurried along the passageway that led from the back porch back to mice warrens. "I'm taking you for that breakfast I promised."

Sam followed Roland until they came to an area under the house that Sam wasn't familiar with. He sensed that they weren't far from the kitchen, but it was in an area of tunnels and passages that he had never been in before.

"Where are we now Roland? I don't know of anywhere to have breakfast around here," Sam said. The area was only dimly lit by some cracks in the floor boards above.

"Not far now Sam, and we'll be sharing breakfast with some friends of yours."

The passage branched out into a wider corridor, with lots of little nooks and crannies. The corridor was bustling with field mice. Many of them were carrying a load of something or rather, most of it food. Sam's nose twitched at all the smells. Lots of different foods, cheeses, nuts, pickles. Sam began to look forward to breakfast.

The field mice called out greetings to him, waving and calling him 'Mr Sam.' Some of the younger pups reached out and touched him, and then ran away giggling.

"Here we are Sam." Roland gestured at dimly lit entrance. "The orphanage. Some of the little chaps you saved would like to say hello," Roland said as he ducked inside waving for Sam to follow.

"Hello Mr Sam," called out a soft voice as he entered the gloomy entrance to the orphanage.

"Hello Michelle," he replied.

"Hello Roland," said Michelle. Roland smiled and produced a large piece of apple from the pocket of his waist coat and passed it to Michelle.

"King Rat asked me to give you this."

Michelle thanked him and took the apple.

"Won't you give the apple to the orphans?" she said. "It only seems right that you get to see their faces when they see fresh fruit."

Roland smiled and shook his head. "You know they are still quite scared of me. Its that whole rat thing. It's Ok. I don't mind. Maybe Sam might like to give it to them?"

"Well, if Sam would care to *honor* us with his presence, then maybe." Michelle looked at Sam. "But they are only field mice Sam, so don't expect perfect manners like you would in a *house* mouse."

She disappeared into the next room. Roland motioned for Sam to follow here.

"I'll leave you here Sam, I've got other things to do while we are here. Wait here for me, and I will be back soon."

Sam followed Michelle through the door. There were several large nests made up and about twenty field mice pups were carefully cleaning the nests and the floor. When Sam came into the room, they all stopped what they were doing and started whispering to each other. Sam saw Timothy in one corner and several of the other pups were patting him on the back. Timothy gave Sam a shy little wave. One of the other pups pushed him forward towards Sam, but he stepped back and looked embarrassed.

"Pups. Listen up pups," Michelle said, clapping her paws together several times. The pups all sat back on their hind legs and were quiet.

"We have a visitor this morning, so please be on your best behavior. Some of you know Sam Mouse. He was the very brave mouse that distracted the cat when some of you got trapped."

Some of the orphans giggled and pointed at Timothy and two of the other mice.

"Now I want you to be on your best behavior. Perhaps Mr Sam will stay and talk to you about what its like to be a writer?"

"I'll go and cut up this apple for them, if you could say something about how important it is to study and work hard, it would be good," Michelle whispered before leaving for the kitchen.

Sam stood up and started to tell the pups how important it was to study hard and to pay attention to spelling and grammar. But the orphans looked bored, and Sam realized that he was boring himself too. He also realized that none of that mattered. Spelling and grammar were important, but being able to tell a story was more important. The bored looks on the orphan's faces let him know that he wasn't telling a story well.

Sam stopped himself mid-sentence, catching himself just before saying that they should always listen to their parents. Which, even Sam knew, would have been a terribly insensitive thing to say to orphans. One of the pups put up her hand and Sam nodded.

"Mr Sam. Are you really going to kill the cat?" she asked.

All the other orphans started whispering and saying, "Yes, tell us how you are going to kill the cat." One of the pups yelled out, "Does cat tail taste good?" and he pretended to bite the tail of the mouse sitting in front of him.

"Well," Sam said. "The thing is, you see, the cat is...well its a cat. And I, well, I'm a mouse."

"A mouse that will kill that cheeky cat," one of the pups yelled out.

"As I was saying..," Sam continued, "I don't know if its actually possible to fight a cat...let alone kill it."

"But your grandfather did. He fought the cat and made it run away. He saved the field mice too."

"Yes", cried another, "we learnt about your grandfather. We learnt how he came and saved the field mice and how he fought the cat."

Michelle came back in with a tray full of cut up apple pieces. The pups went silent when they saw the apple.

"Now pups, line up, one at a time, Mr Sam will give you your piece of apple."

As each orphan came up to Sam, Michelle passed him a piece of apple, and Sam gave the apple to the orphan. Each one politely said, "Thank you Mr Sam," nodding their head, or giving a little bow. Timothy smiled at Sam when he took his piece. None of the pups started eating until all the other pups had a piece of apple. Although Sam could see them eyeing the apple off and licking their lips. There was no apple left over. When the last orphan sat down, they all looked at Michelle, who nodded, and they began gnawing on their apple.

"Slowly, slowly," she said smiling.

"Would you like something to eat Sam?" she asked.

#

"I'm sorry, but this is all we have. If Roland hadn't bought an apple this morning, the kids would have eaten this instead."

Sam looked around the room that passed for the kitchen. It was very bare, the wooden table top was mottled and grey, but it looked like it had been scrubbed. Some pots and pans sat next to the sink. They were battered and old, but very clean.

"That's OK," Sam said, looking at the piece of bread that Michelle had passed to him. It was very hard and stale. As Sam bit into the bread, crumbs exploded everywhere, covering his face in dry bread. Michelle giggled and placed a cup of water in front of him, and he took a sip. She smiled at him in a way that made him feel a little bit foolish and then dunked her piece of bread in the cup in front of her.

"Dunk the bread in your water. Makes it easier to eat," she said. "Softens the bread up a little bit."

Sam tried dipping his bread in the water, and it did indeed soften it up. But now it tasted like soggy stale bread. Sam thought about the pumpernickel and Brie that he often had for breakfast.

"So, does Roland come here often?" Sam asked.

"Once every couple of days, normally with a piece of fruit or cheese for the orphans to share. He really cares for them. Its a little bit sad that they are scared of him. But it doesn't seem to bother him. I think he feels close to the field mice. The rats tolerate him because of his father, but they think of him as a mouse. The house mice see him as a rat. So do the field mice to tell the truth. He scares me a little bit, even though I know he's a good mouse. Or a good rat.

"I feel sorry for him. He doesn't really belong anywhere. But even though the mice are scared of him, he tries to look after them in his own way. Probably because his mother was a field mouse. Or maybe because he knows what its like to be an outsider."

Sam took another bite of the stale bread, dipping it again in the water. It tasted moldy. He tried very hard not to wrinkle his nose up as he ate.

"I know its not what you are used to Sam, but its what the orphans eat every day."

"Don't the orphans like normal food?" Sam asked.

Michelle looked a little bit angry. Sam wondered why everyone seemed to get angry at him so much. Ever since he became a hero. Maybe being a mouse hero wasn't all it seemed to be.

"No Sam," she said. "They would love 'normal' food. Food that you or every other house mouse gets to eat everyday. But that's food that they may get to taste once or twice in their lives. They would love to have something other than soggy bread, or the moldy rind of your leavings. I'd say they dream about a nice piece of cheddar, or a small slurp of milk. Except that some nights they are so hungry, that all they dream about is another piece of soggy bread to fill their bellies."

Michelle started wiping up the crumbs Sam had made when he bit into the bread.

"I'm sorry," Sam said. "I don't know that much about field mice."

"Sam," Michelle said. "You don't understand. Field mice, house mice. There isn't really a difference, other than what we decide is different. You wouldn't like soggy bread or moldy fruit. What makes you think we like it? Because we lived in the fields? Most of us weren't even born in the fields, we were born in the house, same as you. That's the main difference. Where we were born."

"But… But they needn't go hungry. There is plenty of food. I saw foragers returning with food just a few minutes ago when Roland and I came down here. If you need more food, then ask Mr Montagu for more. Just because they are orphans, it doesn't mean that they have to go hungry."

"Sam. You are probably a decent fellow. By all accounts, you are a good mouse. I know you risked your lives to save those orphans. Running onto the cat's head to save Max was the bravest thing I've ever seen. You are obviously a brave mouse. But you don't know very much. That food that the field mice are gathering isn't for the field mice. That goes to the committee, who decide who gets what.

"Its not just the orphans that don't get much. Its ALL the field mice. We get what the house mice don't want. The committee doesn't let the field mice have the nice food. We get the stale food. The rotten food. And when there isn't enough food, we get none. This is the price we pay for living in the house. If we don't like it, then the committee threatens to kick us out of the house."

One of the orphans came in and washed his face and paws in the sink. Michelle made him have a sip of water. Soon the other orphans came in one-by-one. Michelle had a word or two with each one, reminding them of some chore, or homework that needed doing, or asking after a skinned knee or sore paw. Even though the pups were a bit shy around Sam, he could tell that they loved Michelle very much.

"How did you end up looking after the orphans?" Sam asked.

"I don't know," Michelle said, clearing up the last of the breakfast mess. "My parents died when I was young, not long after we came into the house. There was some fighting between the house mice, the field mice and the rats. I don't know much about it, but they were killed. So many field mice died around then, there was no one really to bring me up. The other field mice helped me out, but they were struggling to survive as well, so they couldn't give me much help. I sort of got by and when I was older I decided that no other orphans would have to survive without someone looking after them. I managed to get this apartment set up for orphans, and other field mice and Roland help out when they can.

"The committee agreed to let me look after the orphans, although recently when food became short, Mr Montagu said I had to teach them how to forage earlier than I normally would. That's why we were out the other day."

"I don't understand," Sam said. "Food isn't in short supply. There is plenty to go around."

Michelle smiled at him. "There is only plenty if you are a house mouse. You don't forage anymore. None of the house mice do. Who do you think forages for you? We do. Now that the cat is back, the foraging is getting harder. I think it won't be long before even the house mice will start getting less to eat."

Sam was quiet for some time.

"I didn't realize. I thought the committee just arranged everything," he said.

"They do. They force us to forage, and if we don't then there are consequences. But foraging when the cat is around is very hard, so each trip we take less food, and the committee takes more food off us. Some of the younger field mice are starting to get angry. But Mr Montagu promised that the committee would do something about the cat, and the food would return to normal. That's why we were all very excited when they announced that you would be dealing with the cat."

Michelle made them both a coffee. It was instant coffee and very watery but Sam said it tasted very nice and thanked her for it. She smiled.

"I'm sorry I was rude to you yesterday," Sam said. "I guess I thought I knew a lot more about things than I really do. I'm sorry. That's what I'm trying to say. I'm sorry."

Michelle didn't say anything but she smiled again, which made Sam feel a lot better.

"So Sam, what will you do about the cat? I did think it incredibly brave. The first time you attacked the cat, well, I knew you did it without thinking, but the second time...well, you planned that. Even if it was a bad plan."

"It wasn't my plan," Sam muttered with sigh. "It was the committees' plan."

Chapter Thirteen - The Committee

Sam took the kettle off the stove and started making himself a cup of tea. Before he had gotten very far though, there was a knock at the door. Sam sighed. There was a time when days went by between knocks at the door, and Sam had been very happy about that. Now it seemed that as soon as he made himself a cup of tea, there would be a knock at the door.

Sam didn't even bother saying go away, because the way his life was going at the moment, he knew who ever it was, wouldn't go away. They were as likely to just open the door and walk right in.

Without another knock, the door opened and Damon walked in.

"Hello again Sam. How are you? You look surprisingly good for a chap that's recently been a plaything for an angry cat. Some cat fighting family secret? Wish I had your stamina."

Sam sat down.

"You're a good egg Sam. Honestly, when the committee chose you, I said to myself 'Now there is a poor fellow that's been set to fail'. A veritable Sisy-phus as it were, but you've impressed me no end. A much better mouse than I. Truly."

Sam looked at Damon, not sure what to say.

"I… well, I've tried my best, but I don't know what else to do. I don't know how the committee expects me to fight a cat. I really don't."

"Sam, the committee never expected you to fight the cat. Not successfully anyway. They don't care about the cat at all. The committee just needed to take the attention away from them. Which, they have. Or rather, which you have," Damon said.

"Anyway Sam, I didn't come down to chit chat, as nice as that would be. The committee has sent me down here to ask you to come right away. And when I say ask, they didn't really mean ask. They meant tell. And when I say tell, what I really mean is 'summon'. They want me to tell that you are summoned right away. I've got a formal letter here. All stamped and signed saying that you fail to attend at your own peril."

Sam looked at the letter. It had a very official looking red seal over the opening. He closed his eyes and put the letter on the table.

"No need to read it Sam old chap. Committee wants to speak to you. Best we go. Now."

Sam sighed. "Let me get my coat."

#

Sam stood in front of the committee once again. He still felt very intimidated by the mice staring down at him and the pictures on all the walls. But most of all he was very tired. Three days ago he'd never even been inside the committee room. Nor had he ever met a rat. Nor had he ever fought a cat. Sam didn't know how any of those things had happened to him.

For once, there were other mice in the committee room. No field mice were present, but Sam saw many house mice sitting at the back of the room. Mice he knew. Acquaintances, and neighbors. Sam did not know how they had all heard that this meeting was on, when he had only just found out himself. Sam sniffed the air. He thought he could smell a rat. Literally. He glanced about the small crowd behind him, but couldn't see any rats present. Perhaps Roland was there, but Sam couldn't see him anywhere.

"My dearest Sam," the Mayor said, peering over his spectacles and studying Sam. "I assume you are here to present your report on how you have dealt with the cat. Or should I say, plan to deal with the cat, for it comes to our attention that your plan this evening didn't really succeed and that you ran from the cat. Are we to assume that this beast will now continue to terrorize the community?"

"Well, er... yes, um, you honor, I did indeed have a bit of er... well, a brush so to speak, with the cat, and it didn't go all that well, not well at all really.

But Mr Mayor, I beg your leave to discuss another matter, one of greater importance, if you, um… if you'll permit it that is..."

The mayor leaned even further forward, and adjusted his glasses once more, until Sam thought they would fall off the end of his snout.

"Hmmm, I cannot think what would be more important than the matter of the cat, but go on.... mind you...don't waste any more of our time than you must, for we are all very busy mice you know." The rest of the committee nodded and muttered.

"Mr Mayor... committee members, I have spoken to many good mice, both field and house, the rats, and indeed other animals such as the sugar glider, whom is held in high regard by all who know him. And. Well, it would appear that there is some, well, some discrepancy with how things are handled. I'm sure the committee is doing its utmost. Believes it is doing its utmost, but...well there is some concern that things may not be... well, as fair as they might be.

"You see Mr Mayor", Sam continued, "The field mice are, well, they do a lot of work, perhaps, work that some of the house mice should do. And, well, maybe the committee could review how the whole food situation..," Sam trailed off.

There was silence. The committee members all glanced about, or glared at him, except for Charles, who looked down at the floor in front of him, like a father whose child has done something embarrassing in public.

The Mayor removed his glasses, and made a great show of folding them up and placing them on the desk in front of him. He cleared his throat.

"Now listen here Sam, for I do not intend to repeat myself. You were quite clearly tasked by this most august and wise body of mice to deal with the cat. For some time now we have pondered how you would do this. And pondered. And yet again pondered, whilst you have done NOTHING." The Mayor finished off with a roar, that made Sam take a step back.

"And today," the Mayor continued, quieter now, "you come before us with some rather dreadful accusations that the committee is somehow not looking after the interests of all mice. You, after failing at a very simple task DARE suggest that the committee is not working very hard to solve very difficult problems? You have been very happy to live under the protection of the committee until now. Until you have been asked to contribute to solving the problem. You point to the failings of others to hide your own failings. It is YOU that has failed.

"You whine about food and freedom, yet you fail to take any positive steps to provide that food, or that freedom. The committee has discussed this matter at length. At length Sam. While you have been doing NOTHING, this committee has made several important resolutions on the matter. The field mice are not your concern. The cat is, and I suggest you look to what concerns you, and leave that which does not concern you to those that are wiser than you."

As the mayor concluded, the rest of the committee muttered, 'quite right... young fool.... who does he think he is... seems old Noahs fruit fell far from the tree eh? Not quite the mouse he could be.'

"But Mr Mayor," Sam started, "I've tried to deal with the cat...but I must say, it is a rather big undertaking for just one mouse. I've really no idea how to begin. I've faced the cat twice now, and..."

"ENOUGH," roared the Mayor. "I will not repeat myself. I begin to suspect that the committee has shown an error of judgment in selecting you as the mouse hero, for it appears that you are hesitant to confront the cat...you appear to have an over abundance of caution."

Sam looked around, although he now knew that no support would be forthcoming. His eyes locked with Charles for a moment. Charles appeared to be about to say something, but he looked away, and Sam's heart felt like it had plummeted through the floor. The Mayor glanced around, and many of the mice nodded. He banged his gavel with a precise authority.

"Sam I hear-by charge you, go from here and do not return until you have dealt with the cat, as you have been directed to do. I warn you, should you be delinquent in this matter, do not bother showing your

snout amongst decent mice. You shall be banished.
Sent out of the house unless you deal with this cat." He
banged his gavel again, as if to punctuate the sentence.

Sam nodded, struggling to hold back his emo-
tions. He turned and walked away, fearing that if he
moved too fast, he might run. As he approached the
door, mice moved out of the way, as if fearing to touch
him, none meeting his eyes.

#

Sam sat on the back porch, his feet dangling
over the edge. He looked up and could see the sun's
rays hitting the tops of the trees. He couldn't see Sugar
Glider, but he knew he was up there somewhere, and
the thought made him happy. He munched on a piece
of apple and let his mind go blank. After a while he
sensed someone behind him. He turned. It was Roland.

"Hello Roland," Sam said, and for the first time
seeing Roland made him feel happy, rather than
nervous.

"Hello Sam," Roland said. "You are up early.
I've been watching you some time, but I didn't want to
disturb your meditation."

Sam smiled but said nothing, and for many
minutes they both sat there on the porch enjoying the
peace and quiet in the predawn light. Only after the sun
was fully up did Sam say anything, and it came as a
big surprise to him.

"Roland, I'd like to speak to King Rat again."

152

"Roland, I'd like to speak to King Rat again."

Chapter Fourteen - Another Cat Attack

Sam sat in King Rat's lair. Roland and Sam had travelled through rat territory, unchallenged this time by any other rat. But as they walked through the dark tunnels, Sam saw dark red rat's eyes watching him from the gloom. Roland didn't seem to notice, or if he did, it didn't bother him. Sam was relieved when they left the gloomy dank passageways and entered King Rat's lair. King Rat's lair felt light and safe, even if it was home to the toughest rat of all.

"So Sam, you made quite an impression on everyone yesterday. You've got a taste for cat now have you?" rumbled King Rat.

"No Sir," Sam said. "But somehow I keep finding myself in situations where the only thing I can do is bite the cat. I do everything I can to avoid such situations, but it seems that such situations keep finding me."

Both Roland and King Rat smiled.

"I understand that you were summoned to a committee meeting yesterday. How did it go?" King Rat asked.

"Surely you know?" said Sam. "Roland was there, wasn't he? I mean, I didn't see him, but it was a bit crowded in the room."

"No. I didn't know about the meeting. No one told me," said Roland.

"Oh," said Sam. "I smelt a rat during the meeting. I thought it might have been Roland." But as he said this, he realized that Roland didn't really smell that much like a rat.

King Rat and Roland looked at each other.

"Scar?" said Roland to King Rat. King Rat shook his head.

"No rat should have attended that meeting without telling me. Other than you Roland. If Scar went then he is up to no good. It seems I have some work to do. So Sam, you haven't come to play chess, what brings you here this early in the morning?" King Rat asked.

"What was my grandfather's plan? You said you both worked on a plan? Can you tell me what it was?" Sam asked.

King Rat sighed.

"Mice. They'll be the death of me, either by cat attack or by annoying me with plans and questions about plans. I will tell you Sam, of your grandfather's

plan. But get out of your head any idea of implement-
ing the plan, because it required me to gather more rats
to the cause, and even though I am King Rat, I cannot
make any rat do something that is not in their nature."

King Rat leaned forward and looked directly at
Sam. "Your grandfather's plan was a little bit too
elaborate for my liking. He wanted us lure the cat out
of the kitchen and into the living room. The living
room is filled with so many silly knick knacks. Pieces
of china, plates with pretty pictures on them sitting on
lace doilies. Porcelain dolls sitting on shelves. All
manner of silly and useless stuff.

Your grandfather said that the humans think
these silly things to be of great value."

King Rat leaned back and looked out the window. "The plan was to lead the cat on a merry old
chase, and to duck and weave around these delicate
and precious things. Your grandfather was certain that
the cat would knock over something. Break it, or make
it fall onto the floor.

"But if the cat didn't knock over a piece of glass
or china, then this is where the rats come into it," said
King Rat. "Us Rats, with our bigger bodies and stronger limbs, would run up onto the tables and shelves and
push these stupid pieces of rubbish onto the floor,
where they will break and chip and shatter.

"And when the humans saw the damage done
in their home, then they would take the cat and send it

away, or make it live outside. Or so your grandfather believed.

"I wasn't so sure. I'm still not so sure. These things sometimes have unintended consequences. When you try to control the actions of another for your own benefit, things sometimes backfire on you. That's my experience anyway.

"But your grandfather said that the chance of banishing the cat was worth the risk."

"We could do that," Sam said, getting excited by the idea. "Surely, this would unite the rats and the mice. I can get the committee to support it."

King Rat smiled. "Of course the committee will support it. They will support anything that appears to be dealing with the cat. My concern Sam is that even if I can convince the rats to help, will it actually work? Will the cat be banished? What if the cat isn't banished? Then what? Its not really a good plan at all."

Sam and King Rat argued back and forth about how the plan would work.

"OK Sam. You haven't convinced me that the plan will work, but I will try. I will try because your grandfather believed as passionately as you do that this plan would work. But I warn you, even when you get what you want, sometimes what you want, isn't what you need."

As Sam got up to leave, King Rat coughed quite badly, and it took a minute or two before he stopped. As Sam reached the door, King Rat called out. "This is a dangerous undertaking Sam. Someone could die. Are you ready for that? Do you fear death Sam?"

"Of course I do. I don't want to die."

"I've been thinking about it a lot lately. I've come to appreciate death."

"Appreciate death? How can you appreciate death? Why would you want to die?." said Sam

"I never said you should want to die, I said you should appreciate death. If you *really* know that you are going to die, you will live every day and enjoy it. You would not waste it. Life is short and unpredictable. Short for a rat. Even shorter for a mouse. If you really understood that, then you would not be wasting your time worrying about things that you cannot control, and you would fill every available moment with living. Focus on what you can control, and learn to live with those things you cannot control. Trying to control things that are beyond your control is a path to unhappiness."

"I tell you this, because I think that your intentions are noble, but I do not believe your cause is right. It is not the cat that is the problem. Do not waste your life on unimportant things Sam, it would be a shame to face the cat and realize that you had never truly lived your life as it was meant to be lived."

#

Sam stood in the shadow of the hole that lead out into the kitchen floor. The cat was asleep in the center of the floor. He looked down the passageway to where a number of other mice were sitting watching him. His heart was beating fast and he could feel his stomach tighten when he thought about what he and the other mice were about to do.

Roland stood next to him. Sam was glad to have him so close.

Michelle came up to them. "Please be careful Sam, I know you are very brave, but please be very careful. I would hate to lose you." She gave Sam a little hug and then scurried off. Sam was surprised. He added Michelle to the list of people that would care if he got hurt.

"You ready Sam?" Roland asked. Sam nodded.

Mr Montagu and Gypsy strolled up. Mr Montagu nodded to Roland. "Well Sam. Don't cock this one up eh?"

"Try not to run away this time Sam," Gypsy said.

Sam realized that Gypsy was never on the list of people who cared what happened to him.

"Its time," said Roland. Roland scampered out into the kitchen, and Sam followed straight after him. Straight towards the sleeping cat.

#

Roland ran wide, out to the right of the cat, Sam ran off to the cat's left side. Sam's mouth was very dry, and his heart was beating wildly. So wildly, that it sounded like a machine humming away. As he got closer to the cat, he realized that it wasn't his heart beating that he could feel, but the deep purring of the cat. Sam stopped. He looked across to make sure Roland was in position. This was the most dangerous time. If the cat woke up too soon, it could all be over for Sam.

Roland raised his paw and waved. Sam could hardly see him, with the bulk of the cat laying between them. Sam took a deep breath. He could see himself, running at the cat, up its front paw, onto its head, where he would bite its ear, before running straight down the other paw, towards Roland. The cat would chase after them both, angry at being bitten for a third time. Roland was there to help Sam if he slipped, or if the cat was too fast. They would both run into the living room, where the rats were positioned to start pushing over pieces of china and plates. In the confusion, Sam and Roland would slip under a bookshelf in the living room until the coast was clear. Sam could see it all unfolding clearly in his mind.

Sam took a deep breath and ran straight at the cat. He was almost on the cat's paw, bracing himself to run up the beasts leg, when one of the cats eyes opened. The cat sat bolt upright, too quickly for a sleeping cat.

The cat sat upright, both eyes fixed on Sam, a loud hiss coming from its mouth. Sam tried to stop, but he just fell over and skidded across the floor straight towards the cat's paw. He bumped into one paw before coming to a stop, laying flat on his back. Before he could move, the cat bought a single paw down on top of him, pinning him down. Sam could hardly breathe. Each time he let out a bit of air, the cat pushed down harder. Sam's vision started to go black.

Just as he thought he was about to lose con-sciousness, the cat lifted the paw off him, and Sam drew in a huge breath. His vision started to clear, and Sam knew he had to get on his feet or the cat would be upon him. He struggled to get up, trying to focus on where the cat was.

He was knocked sideways as the cat batted at him with the other paw. Sam felt a hard whack, and he slide far across the kitchen floor, spinning and tum-bling as he went. He came to a sudden stop with a thud as he hit a skirting board, but the slide across the floor had given a moment to catch his breath. Sam felt himself being pulled to his feet.

"Get up Sam, no time to be laying around."

Roland pulled Sam to his feet. By chance, the cat had hit Sam towards the door into the lounge room. Sam looked at the cat. It seemed surprised to see two rodents on the floor, and it hesitated before lowering itself into a crouch.

"We've got to get to the lounge room Sam," Roland said, tugging Sam towards the door. "Run Sam, Run."

For the third time in as many days, Sam ran.

#

Sam looked up as he ran into the lounge room. He could hear Roland behind him, and the cat not far behind. Sam's legs were burning from running so hard, and his breath was pounding through his lungs. As he entered the living room, he heard King Rat yell at him, "Don't look back.". Sam glanced around and saw King Rat standing beside the door. Sam kept running until he was in the center of the living room.

"I'm right behind you. Keep going," yelled Roland from behind him.

Sam ran, his lungs aching from the bruising and from running so hard. Behind him he could hear the cat pounding on the floor boards. The pounding stopped, and there was a loud and terrible hissing and squealing. Against his better judgment, Sam looked back again and saw that the cat had stopped chasing them, and was now spinning around. The cat was spinning around so fast it looked like a typhoon of fur crossing the lounge floor. Sam caught a glimpse of King Rat, holding on to the cat's tail, and he could hear King Rat laughing hard and yelling, "Is that the best you can do you pussy?"

Roland and Sam both stopped near the bookcase and watched, mesmerized by the spinning ball of cat and rat. Sam's breath returned and the aching in his ribs became a dull all over throbbing.

"Should we do something?" he asked.

Roland shook his head.

"What? Not sure what we can do. The cat will stop soon enough. If we try to get close, we'll just get knocked over."

Right at that moment King Rat let go of the cats tail and with a gleeful, "Wheeee" he slid head first across the floor coming to a stop at Sam's feet. He shook his head and looked up at Sam.

"Well, that was a lot of fun," he said.

"No time to boast father, the cat is coming."

King Rat smiled and pointed to the bookshelf above them.

"Roland, my dear boy, fear not. For the rats have got us covered. All those lovely pieces of china shall soon come tumbling down. But we should move out of the way, else we will get a dainty piece of china on our heads."

They scurried underneath the bookcase. The gap under the bookcase was big enough that the cat could probably get to them with its paws, but long before that became a problem, china and glassware would descend on the cat, and if not hitting it, at least startling it enough that it would lose interest in the three rodents underneath the book case.

The cat stopped spinning and spotted them just as they got under the cover of the bookshelf. It stalked towards them, eyes darting around to make sure it knew where all the possible escape routes were. Sam had never seen an animal look angrier, and yet cold at the same time. There was no doubt that the cat was going to kill anything it got its hands on.

King Rat laughed.

"That kitty cat is in for a big surprise when the rats start pushing plates down."

The cat reached the bookshelf and put its head down against the gap beneath the lowest shelf. The gap wasn't big enough for the cat to fit under, but it jammed its face close to them. Sam could feel its hot fishy breath washing over him. The cat just stared, first at King Rat, then at Roland and finally at Sam.

Like lightning, a paw thrust forward and then swept underneath the bookshelf. The three rodents jumped back just out of reach of the cat's paw.

King Rat taunted the cat.

"Silly Beast, you're just a cat,

While I'm the king of the Rats,

You can't catch me,

nor these friends you see,

You're a stupid moggy,

But soon, you'll be,

Outside with the doggy."

"I didn't think there was a dog outside?" said Roland.

"There isn't but it sort of rhymed, so I went with it," King Rat replied.

The cat swiped its paw in again. This time it managed to stretch further in, and though they all jumped clear, Sam felt the cat's long claws brush past him, so close that he saw some of his hair falling to the floor.

"Father," Roland cried out.

Sam looked and saw that there was a long seam of blood oozing out of King Rat's belly.

"I'm all right, just a surface scratch. But next time he'll be closer, he's got our range."

The cat was inspecting the end of its paw, and Sam could see a glistening of blood on one claw, and tufts of hair on the others. The cat smiled and pointed one claw at Sam and winked.

"Where are those damn rats?" King Rat said, "there should be an avalanche of plates and glasses right now. Someone is going to have to go and check and see what they are up to."

"If we all stay together, the cat only has to watch one spot," said Roland. "We need to all stand separately, so the cat has to watch all of us. If we split up and run around the cat will have to work harder to keep up."

Without another word, they moved apart. Sam and Roland worked their way down to one end of the bookcase, while King Rat moved to the other end. The cat watched for a moment and then moved down to Sam's end of the bookcase.

"Stupid Cat, hates me more than anyone," grunted Sam as they dodged another sweep of the paw. Roland looked back and gave a thumbs up to King Rat at the other end of the bookcase. Sam couldn't see King Rat, he was too busy keeping an eye on the cat.

"He's gone to find out why the plates aren't coming down," said Roland.

For the next few minutes Sam and Roland run back and forth dodging the cat. They were both tiring fast. With only a little movement the cat could reach anywhere under the bookcase, and could keep the rodents continually running.

Roland and Sam now sported a number of minor scratches, and Sam knew it was only a matter of time before one of them got more than a minor scratch.

The cat was getting faster and faster with its swipes, coming from the left then the right, sometimes so fast that it appeared like it was using both front paws at once.

Something dropped from above, landing next to the cat with a small ringing sound. It rolled under the bookcase and came to rest. The cat stopped for a second and stared at it. So did Roland and Sam. It was a ceramic thimble, covered in fine paintings of roses.

The cat gave a startle as something else came tumbling down, this time landing on its back. It was another ceramic thimble, this one with paintings of Siamese cats on it. Several more quickly followed, some landing on the cat. Others landing on the floor with a with a clatter. At first the thimbles distracted the cat, but after the third one landed on it, the cat focused back again on Sam and Roland.

"That's it?" Roland asked. "We are going to get the cat with thimbles?"

Another thimble came tumbling down, and it rolled in under the bookcase. The cat gave another swipe at Roland and Sam. Sam took cover behind the thimble, but it went sliding across the floor when the cat hit it.

"We should split up, make it harder for the cat," Sam grunted as he watched the thimble slide to a stop. But they didn't, and Sam was glad of Roland's company.

There was a loud crash, and instead of dodging the cat's paws, Sam and Roland had to duck as shards of porcelain showered them and the cat.

"A plate," yelled Roland.

The cat seemed a bit more shook up this time. Another plate followed, this time landing on the other side of the cat. The cat stepped back from the book-shelf, forgetting Roland and Sam for the moment, staring up at the shelves above it. A third plate came down, smashing into pieces, with a big piece landed on the cat's tail. The cat gave a startled shriek, and then leapt up onto the bookshelf. Suddenly plates, cups, thimbles and even ornamental teaspoons came crash-ing down around Sam and Roland.

Roland laughed. "Let's go. I'd hate to survive the cat only to be killed by falling bric-a-brac."

They ran out from under the bookcase, following the wall. When they got to the other side of the room, they could see the cat pouncing around on the bookshelf, smashing plates and cups onto the ground. There didn't appear to be any rats up there, just the cat. Across the room, up on the coffee table Sam saw some small mice pushing leaning up again a photo frame, pushing it back and forth. With each push the picture frame rocked a bit closer to the edge of the table. With one last push, picture frame fell from the table, and smashed on the floor sending fragments of glass flying across the room.

"Field mice," Sam said. "Look, there are field mice on the table, and over there, on the mantel piece."

Sure enough, on the mantel piece there was a collection of snow globes, and one of the globes was sliding slowly towards the edge. It fell with a great crash, sending a shower of water and glitter across the Persian rug beside the fire place.

"I think that's a job well done, that cat's in trouble now," said Sam.

"I think the rats are in trouble too." Roland replied. "I can't see a single one, its all field mice up there. But where are the rats?"

#

Sam stood on the kitchen window sill. He'd never stood there before. There was a small hole in the window slider that allowed a mouse to squeeze out from inside the wall onto the kitchen window sill. But few mice ever came here, for it was dangerous, and there was no reason to come here. Today though, the mice got to stare out the window at the cat. It was raining, and the cat sat on the window ledge glaring in at the mice. Water ran down its whiskers. It looked very unhappy.

Sam had bought the orphans up here as a treat. They were laughing and pointing and making fun of the cat.

"Ok pups," Michelle said, frowning. "I know its a nasty old cat, but let's not make fun of another animal's misfortune. Time to go."

The pups all complained and groaned, but followed her instructions, slipping by one-by-one.

'Don't make them rush too much. They deserve this moment," said Sam. "If it weren't you, the orphans, and the other field mice, Roland and I would have been cat food."

Michelle smiled, but still shooed all the pups through the crack into the safety of the wall. Sam was the last one through. He paused, looking back at the miserable wet cat, still glaring at him. He almost felt sorry for the cat, now that it was all over with. Almost.

Sam gave the cat a friendly wave before he pulled himself through the crack in the window slider.

Chapter Fifteen - Final Confrontation

The door closed and Sam carried in the large hamper full of fruit and cheese that had just been delivered. He set it on the floor. There was a card, Sam couldn't make out the writing, but could see that it was Gypsy's hand writing.

"A peace offering?" Roland asked. Sam smiled at his friend.

"Maybe," Sam replied. "Can I make you another tea?"

Roland shook his head.

"Aren't you going to open it Sam?"

"No," Sam paused for a moment. "I rather think I would like to take it down to the orphans tomorrow for their breakfast."

"Oh...Gypsy won't like you giving such nice food to the field mice," said Roland, a big grin covering his face.

Sam grinned back. "No. I would like to see her face when she finds out."

The two friends laughed, and then settled down into quiet contemplation while they finished their morning tea.

"So," Sam asked. "What actually happened with the rats?"

"Scar convinced them not to turn up. Well some of them. Most of the rats remained loyal to my father, but Scar told them that there had been a change of plan and that King Rat didn't need their help anymore. We haven't seen Scar since, but the damage is done. I think there will be a challenge soon from Scar, or another rat. My father might win. Or he might not. I don't know."

"We were very lucky that the field mice were able to help out," said Sam.

"Not luck Sam. Michelle was very smart. She could see that the rats weren't in place, if she hadn't rushed the orphans and other field mice up to the bookcase and tables in the living room, you and I might not be here to celebrate."

There was an urgent flurry of knocks at the door, and the door burst wide open. It was Damon. "Sam, old chap. No time to talk. Emergency meeting of the committee. I think you should be there.

Oh...hello Roland. I think you should probably come as well. Come, no time to talk." Damon turned to go.

"Wait up Damon, what's the rush?"

Damon turned around. "The Mayors dead. They are saying it might be murder."

#

For the third time in his life Sam stood in the committee room. Apart from the committee members, Sam, Roland and Damon were the only other mice present. The Mayor's seat was empty.

Charles Montagu had a gavel in his hand, which he banged once before speaking. "Well, as senior committee member, I shall run this meeting until another mayor is elected, Winston, have you a report to present on the Mayor's death?"

"Indeed I have," said the elderly mouse, shuffling some papers before clearing his throat. "Mr Montagu, fellow committee members, and, umm..." Winston glanced at Sam, Roland and Damon, "and advisors, I have made an extensive examination of the circumstances surrounding the Mayor's death. As you know, the Mayor receives the pick of the food. Its one of the privileges of being Mayor. One of 'perks' of the job as it were. Unfortunately, it may have been the Mayor's downfall. You see, the blue stilton that the Mayor ate. It would seem that it was poisoned."

There were intakes of breath around the room. Charles tapped his gavel.

"And, Winston, do you have any clue as to who may have done such a terrible thing?" Charles looked straight at Roland and then at Sam when he said this.

"Yes Mr Montagu. I do believe that the food was poisoned by the humans. Now that the cat is gone, I do believe that they will take to poisoning some items in the pantry. After all, since the cat left, we've raided the pantry very heavily indeed. They were bound to notice, and bound to take action."

The room burst into conversations and shouted questions. "is our food safe?" cried one committee member. "How do we know if its poisoned?" said another. Charles banged his gavel again.

"Silence please. As minister for food, I can assure you of several things. Firstly, every step possible will be taken to ensure that the mice receive good healthy food. In fact, I have, just in case mind you, had a plan prepared for such an eventuality for some time. May I have the committee's leave to present this plan now?"

All the members nodded agreement.

"Very well, " continued Charles. "As you know for some time there has been growing resentment from the field mice that the food they receive may not be to the same standard as what the house mice receive, and it is a perception only might I point out, but for some time there has been growing anger among those wretched field mice about their food. We have known for some time that this would become a problem.

"And now we have this poisoning problem. Well, one problem offers us the solution to the other problem. Tomorrow, I will publicly announce that a review has been undertaken by my department into food distribution, and from this day forth, all food will be evenly distributed among field mice and house mice."

"That's all well and good," interjected one committee member, "it will keep the field mice happy. But how does it help with the poison?"

Winston frowned. "Charles, are you proposing that we use the field mice to test our food?"

"Well, that's a horrible notion Winston, but, what I do suggest is that we distributed every day's foraging to the field mice first. It's only fair that they get the freshest food, surely? After all, they risk their lives foraging for us, shouldn't we show our gratitude by letting them have the food first? Only after, maybe the next day, will we distribute to the house mice. Its fair after all."

The committee members all nodded in agreement, and someone started clapping, and soon the committee were all clapping.

Sam looked at Roland. Roland's face was dark and angry, but Roland shook his head slowly when Sam looked at him. Sam wasn't sure why.

"Mr Montagu," Sam shouted, so as to be heard above the committee members clapping. "Surely, you are not suggesting that we use the field mice to see if the food is poisoned, before the house mice eat it? But that's terrible... you cannot do that... I won't let you do that, and the other house mice won't either."

Charles banged his gavel hard.

"Sam Mouse. This is a secret emergency committee meeting, and we are discussing things way beyond your understanding. Leave now. You were only present because there was some suspicion that YOU may have some knowledge of the Mayor's death. Damon, take Sam back to his apartment, and see that he talks to no one until he calms down."

Damon grabbed Sam and whispered in his ear, "Not now Sam, old boy, come with me." Sam started protesting, but Damon was quite firm and with Roland by his side they marched him down to his apartment without another word.

"Roland," Damon said. "I must get back to the committee. We need to know what they are planning next. Keep you little friend quiet please until we know what's going on."

Roland nodded. Sam was almost in tears as Roland closed the apartment door behind them.

"How can you support them?" Sam yelled at Roland. "How can you just keep quiet?"

"Sam. Be quiet." Roland hissed. "Do you think the committee will let you tell the field mice of their plan? The committee will lock you up to keep you quiet. You will end up being charged with the Mayor's death if you are not careful. Our only hope is to be seen to agree with the committee. I must go talk with King Rat, and then we will come up with a plan. Until then, keep quiet and stay in your apartment. If they question you, agree with everything they say."

There was a hard knock at the door. Roland opened it. A shadow fell across the door. Outside, Sam could see the hulking frame of a very large rat.

"Hello Roland," said Scar. "I've come to have a little talk to Sam."

#

Roland slammed the door shut. "Is there another way out?" he asked.

"No," said Sam. "I only have a front door."

There was a loud thumping on the front door.

"Why is he here?" Sam said.

Roland leaned back against the door to stop Scar from pushing it in. Behind Roland, Sam could see the door bulging each time Scar pounded on it.

"I'm not sure, but it can be for no good reasons. I think the committee wants to keep you quiet Sam. They don't trust you to keep your mouth shut about the poison and their plan to use the field mice to test the food first. The committee has probably got some sort of deal with Scar. That's why the rats didn't turn up yesterday. If Scar thinks he can come here and threaten you, it means that he knows that King Rat can't stop him now. I need to get to King Rat and warn him," said Roland.

"And I have to warn the field mice," said Sam.

The door thumped again. "Open up Sam Mouse, or I'll smash your door down," Scar yelled through the door.

Sam whispered in Roland's ear. Roland shrugged his shoulders.

"Hey Scar," Roland called out. "My mother might have been a field mouse, but your mother had fleas and your father was a mole."

Scar roared with rage and slammed against the door hard. Roland wrenched the door open just as Scar slammed into it. Scar fell at their feet. Sam and Roland ran over the top of Scar and out the door, pausing only to pull the door shut.

"That won't slow him for long" yelled Roland as the ran down the passageway. They both ran on for a minute, but there was no sound of pursuit.

"I'm almost more worried now that Scar isn't chasing us. Sam, I need to go warn my father. You keep going. Warn the field mice as soon as possible. They may already be giving the food out to the field mice."

Sam nodded and they both went their separate ways. As he ran towards the quarters where the field mice lived, Sam's mind was on fire. The field mice might listen to him. But he didn't know what he was going to say.

#

Michelle stared at Sam for a moment, and then sat down. "And that's it. That's what the committee plans to do?"

Max came running in to the orphanage, calling out, "Michelle Michelle." He skidded to a halt.

"Not now Max," She said, "I'm sorry, but Sam and I are talking about something very important."

"But Michelle...you need to come and look," said Max.

"Not now Max," she said.

"Ok, I'll come back in a minute." Max shrugged before disappearing into the orphan's dormitory.

"We have to tell everyone, Sam." Michelle said, in a low voice to avoid the orphans overhearing. "We have to let the committee know that the field mice won't stand for it. Surely the house mice don't want this."

"They won't listen," Sam said. "I don't think the house mice want any field mice hurt, but I don't think they want to give up their food, they don't want to have to forage for themselves. As long as they can pretend it's the committee's problem, and the committee can tell them that the field mice are being ungrateful or paranoid, then the average mouse will be happy. I don't think they will do anything. And then there is the rats."

"King Rat and Roland have always been good to the field mice. The committee will listen to Roland," Michelle said.

"No. The committee *uses* Roland. But he doesn't trust them either. As for King Rat. I think he has enough on his hands dealing with Scar. I think Scar and the committee have some sort of deal going on."

Max came out of the dormitory, with half a dozen other orphans, all chattering excitedly.

"Behave you pups," Michelle called out as they headed towards the front door.

"Come with us Michelle. We are going to the food store," called back the littlest, "They are giving away food, the good stuff."

Sam and Michelle looked at each other. Before he could even react, Michelle was out the door, calling back the orphans. With a great deal of protesting from the pups Sam and Michelle managed to get the orphans back into the orphanage.

"Sam... you must go tell them. You must stop them right away. They will listen to you, everyone here admires you."

"Come with me," he said and she nodded.

#

Sam stood on a little crate in the wide passage-way. It was the largest area available in the cramped burrows of the field mice. The field mice were all packed in tight. Some were muttering among them-selves. Some were crying.

Sam called out to the crowd. "Please, listen to me. If you stay here you will have to deal with the committee. The house mice won't support you. The rats might not be able to help you."

One of the younger field mice yelled out, "Well, we'll forage for ourselves then, and give none of it to the stupid house mice." He picked up a stick and shook it and yelled. "Let them try and take our food. I'll give them a whacking they'll not forget."

Some of the younger mice around him cheered and clapped him on the back.

Roland came running in from the rear of the passageway, pushing his way forward. The field mouse all clapped him on the back as he went.

"Roland's here. He'll not talk about running away," someone yelled. "With Sam, Roland and King Rat on our side, the committee won't be able to make us do anything."

"Sam," Roland hissed in a low whisper when he made his way to where Sam stood. "Scar just challenged King Rat for the title of pack leader. It didn't turn out very well. Scar is now the King of the Rats."

Sam felt a wave of anger wash over him, then concern. "Where is he...where is your father? Is he all right?"

Roland shook his head and Sam could see tears in his eyes.

"He wouldn't give up. I tried to help him, but he knew things were going to go bad. Sam. He told me to tell you to take those field mice that will listen and go. He said you must go and find a nice place by the river in the woods, and that he wished he could have come with you."

Sam was shocked. He couldn't believe King Rat was gone. All around him there was a buzz of conversation as the word passed that King Rat was dead.

"Sam. He gave me these to give to you. Asked you to find somewhere nice for them." Roland passed Sam a cloth. Sam opened it and wrapped up inside were two chess pieces. The King in the shape of a rat and the Queen in the shape of a field mouse. Sam folded them back up.

There was a commotion at the far end, yelling and angry voices. Sam looked up and saw the bulky forms of several rats pushing their way forward. One of them was Scar.

"Right-O," yelled Scar. "There is a new order in charge now. Mr Montagu has sent me down here to get you lazy field mice back to work. And we're here to arrest certain trouble makers. Sam Mouse, Roland Half-Rat and Michelle Den-Mother, you are all under arrest for murder, treason against the committee and your fellow mice."

The rats started to push forward hitting and kicking the field mice as they went. The young fellow with the stick raised his stick as if to hit Scar. Scar laughed and yanked the stick out of his hands, snapped it in two, and hit the young field mouse on the nose with the broken bits. The young field mouse fell down with a wail, blood gushing from his snout.

"Run Sam," said Roland. "Take Michelle and any who will follow. Go to the back porch, and get ready to lead the field mice away. Don't stop to get anything, just go. I'll be right behind. I'm going to slow Scar down." Before Sam could stop him, Roland was gone.

The passageway was chaos. Sam yelled out for the field mice to follow him. Some looked up and pushed towards him, jamming the passageway even more. Others, seeing the confusion, went down side passages trying to get to safety. Michelle grabbed Sam's paw and dragged him inside the entrance to the orphanage, closing the door behind them.

"All right Pups," she called out to those pups that were inside the orphanage. "We are going to take a little trip. You all know Sam right? He's the mouse hero that fought that cat three times and won. We are going to follow him. Now, its very busy outside, so I want you to all stay close. I will come last with some of the older pups."

Michelle nodded to Sam, who opened the door and pushed out. The chaos was even worse as the rats continued to push through the crowded corridors, slowed down by their size, and the number of field mice who were pushing back. Roland was rallying some of the field mice, dragging boxes and furniture out of apartments to slow the rats down. Sam could hear Scar bellowing away, and the occasional cheer of the field mice as they threw pieces of food at the rats. Taking advantage of the confusion, Sam led the orphans away towards the tunnels that lead to the back steps. Soon field mice were coming out of side passages and doorways and following him. Some were empty handed, or holding the hands of their loved ones and pups, but others had boxes and bags and handfuls of clothes and food. As more joined the procession, Sam started tapping the older mice on the shoulders, asking them to take an orphan with them. Sam couldn't tell how many were behind him in the passageway, but he could only just make out Michelle in the distance. She waved at him to push on.

Sam came to the crack in the foundations that opened out onto the back steps. He stuck his head out. It was broad day light, and a light gentle breeze made the trees and grass wave back and forth.

Sam looked out across the short freshly cut back lawn. He saw the cat, far off by the kitchen window asleep in the sun, facing the other way. He turned and motioned for the mice behind him to keep quiet. He stepped out onto the porch. It seemed so much more exposed in the mid-day sun.

Michelle came out and stood next to him. "Oh...I've never been here before."

"Sam, its beautiful. Is that where we are going? She pointed to the distant long grass and the woods beyond.

Sam didn't know. But he knew that they couldn't stay here. He thought about all his things sitting in his apartment. His typewriter, and all the notes he'd prepared on his grandfather, and his comfy nest and his arm chair. And cheese. The lovely pieces of cheese. But he knew that he couldn't have those things if it cost the lives of another mouse.

"Stay here," he said to Michelle. "Keep everyone back, I'm going to go check out the long grass and see what is over there."

"Sam," Michelle said, stopping him before he ran off. "I know you are giving up a lot for us. Please be careful..."

Without looking back, Sam dashed across the lawn. He thought again of his things. His possessions. *They are just things. Grandfather always said the key to happiness was not getting more things, but desiring less things.*

Chapter Sixteen - Leaving The House

Sam scouted the long grass. It was long enough that the mice would be protected from above, and there was a small bush that provided very good shelter. The mice could gather inside the shrub and check that everyone was OK.

Sam dashed back across the lawn and onto the back step. He darted back and forth between shadows to avoid being spotted. He slipped back into the small crack and found it crammed with mice. As his eyes adjusted to the gloom, he tried to see how many there were, but the narrow passageway was crammed as far as he could see.

"How many?" he said to Michelle.

"I don't know Sam, but a lot. The word has passed, there are even house mice here. Mice that heard about what is happening and heard what you are doing."

Sam peered into the gloom, he saw a crowd of faces; expectant some, scared others, but with sudden clarity, Sam realized that what he saw beneath it all was hope. His mouth was very dry. He didn't know if deserved the hope and trust he could see in their eyes. He didn't even know what waited in the woods. But they couldn't stand up to the rats and the rest of the house mice, and Sam didn't know where else they could go.

At the front of all those mice stood Michelle, her whiskers quivering, but her eyes were bright and excited.

"Show us the way Sam," she whispered in his ear, and she gave him a gentle kiss on the cheek. So soft he could not tell when then the kiss began or ended, but as soft as it was, he felt its touch more than any other kiss in his life.

Sam turned to view the openness of the back yard. With a deep breath he stepped outside. A breeze gently ruffled his fur and he smiled and pointed to the long grass on the far side of the yard.

"There," he said, pointing across to the long grass on the edge of the yard.

"Hurry across. Guide everyone across and hide underneath that shrub." He pointed to two of the larger mice. "You first, I'll stay here and make sure the rest get across." The two fellows looked around and then scurried across to the other side. Sam watched as they disappeared into the long grass. After a few seconds one of them reappeared and nodded to Sam.

Sam waved to the next cautious face peering out of the gloom. The first of the field mice stepped out, and then another, and another, and soon there was a stream of tawny colored mice running across the yard. Michelle paired up the older orphans with the younger ones, and managed to find an adult to help them across. Sam watched as even house mice held paws with orphaned field mice, running across the grass together.

"Oh Sam," Michelle said, squeezing his arm. "You did it."

Sam pointed back to the hole where several of the young mice peered out, their noses twitching as they smelt the fresh spring air.

Michelle giggled. "They've never been outside before." She darted over and started reassuring the young mice.

"Come on, I'll take you to the other side." She grabbed the smallest mouse by the paw and said to the other two "Quickly, and we will be across the lawn and in the grass in a flash. Sam is watching, and he'll make sure we get across safely." Sam stood there, watching mouse after mouse making the dash across the lawn. For the first time he understood what it meant to feel satisfaction, what it meant to feel pride. All those days living in his safe little hole with people who he thought where his friends, he realized that he hadn't been living, merely existing. It was like he could suddenly feel the blood pulsing through his body, feel the life inside of him.

A cloud passed over the sun and then another cloud passed over, and Sam looked up, and saw the graceful shape of a hawk, wheeling over the trees. With a sudden angling of its wing, the hawk dropped sharply, ducking behind a tree, and then reappearing on the other side, gliding with its wings back, gathering speed. Gliding straight at the stream of mice, the hawk briefly touched the lawn and then with a rapid beat of its wings launched itself towards the blue sky.

Sam gasped in horror, as he saw a field mouse hanging from the hawk's talons, struggling to break from the cruel needle like claws.

Sam ran out onto the lawn, yelling for the mice to hurry. Many heard him, or had already seen the hawks, and they broke into a run towards the shelter of the long grass. Sam's eyes darted around as he saw another dark shape wheeling above, and then with a slow graceful gliding turn, the next hawk angled down, diving towards the mice below.

"No," gasped Sam as the hawk swooped down and carried off a second mouse. Crying the mouse thrashed about as the hawk's wings clawed at the air, gaining height with every beat. Sam looked and saw three orphans standing in the middle of the lawn, crying.

"Run," Sam yelled at them, running himself to try to reach them. But they just stood there crying. Sam ran out and grabbed one of the pups.

"Where is Michelle?" he cried

The field mouse pup was sobbing so hard that he couldn't say a word, but he was pointing up into the sky.

Sam's heart felt like it had stopped. He looked up and saw the underneath of the hawk. Its cruel beak reaching for the sky. Its sharp talons held a struggling mouse. And Sam could see that it was Michelle. He could see her, fighting against the hawk's clutch. The talons wrapped around her, clutching her tightly.

Sam stood rooted to the ground. Everything seemed to stop. He could hardly hear the cries of the three pups, or the whooshing flap of the hawk's wings. All he could feel was Michelle's kiss on his cheek. Above the climbing hawk, another dark shape came into view, sweeping around the oak tree in a broad graceful arc.

Almost all of the mice had crossed over, leaving just Sam and the three pups in the middle. Pushing Michelle out of his mind, he tried to drag the pups across the lawn to the safety of the grass, but they were so terrified that they just stood there staring at the sky, sobbing. One of pups cried out, Sam looked up and saw a furry winged creature fly right into the hawk that had taken Michelle, smashing into it, grabbing onto it with all four of its paws.

"Sugar Glider," Sam cried out.

Sugar Glider, Michelle and the hawk all thudded to the ground in front of Sam in a heap. The hawk let go of Michelle and started raking its claws across Sugar Glider's face, struggling to get free, but Sugar Glider had the hawk in a tight grip. Sam took hold of Michelle, dragging her clear of the still struggling and screeching hawk.

"Run Sam," shouted Sugar Glider. Sam looked at him in horror. Sugar Gliders face was covered in blood and as he watched, the hawk ran its talons across Sugar Gliders face again, coming away bloody.

"Get. Her. Free. Run," Sugar Glider said, grunting between each word.

Several other mice ran out of the safety of the grass and grabbed the three orphans and carried them to safety. Sam dragged Michelle into the long grass. The last thing he saw of Sugar Glider was him rolling around on the lawn, clutching onto the hawk, while it tried to break free..

#

Sam dragged Michelle deeper into the grass. Several mice came forward and helped him carry her. A short distance into the grass and they reached the relative safety of the small bush. Sam knelt down. Michelle was staring at him, eyes open but not properly focused.

"Sam," she whispered. "Are they all right? Are the orphans here?"

Sam looked up and saw Max, who nodded, and the older mice moved back to allow the orphans to huddle closer. Sam noticed that she was laying oddly and her breathing was shallow and fast.

"They are all here. Safe."

"Thank you Sam.   I wish we had met earlier Sam. I wish we had met some other time." She grabbed Sam's paw and held it.

"So sad," Michelle whispered. She didn't say another word and a few minutes later Sam felt her paw relax and fall out of his grasp.

Sam wept. Big deep sobs that shook his body. All around him he could feel the orphans moving closer, reaching out to touch Michelle, and to touch Sam. There was a rustling in the under growth and all the mice froze, but it was only Roland.

"Hey, I gave that hawk a good thumping before it flew away...but the rats are coming, we'd better hurry," he called out as he came skidding into the undergrowth. "Poor old Sugar Glider he looks pretty beat up..." Roland stopped as he saw the mice gathered around Michelle, and without another word he sat down and put his head in his paws and started shaking his head and crying.

Chapter Seventeen - Field Mice

Samuel scampered up the river bank. This was the furthest he had ever gone from his home, and the burrows of the other mice in his community. His mother did not like him exploring this far away, but when he played near the burrows, the other pups would tease him without mercy. He could move quite fast despite his bad leg, but he had an odd way of walking, and, as you know, young mice can be very cruel to anyone that appears different.

When they weren't staggering around pretending to walk with a lame leg, they teased him about his name. Everyone knew that Samuel was named after Sam, the bravest mouse that had ever lived. All the young mice knew the stories about how Sam had fought the cat, and rescued the mice from a horrible end, and bought them to the river bank to live by the field. So it struck the other young mice that it was very funny that a crippled mouse would be named after such a hero.

In many ways, making fun of his name hurt Samuel more than anything else. His mother told him that 'sticks and stones would break his bones, but names could never hurt him' but Samuel knew that wasn't true. Names were very powerful, and names could hurt a lot. He would rather the sticks and stones.

When the mice played games, even those mice that were his friends didn't want him on their team, because he slowed them down. It was even worse when they did sometimes ask him to play, because Samuel knew they didn't really want him. So when the few mice he did call friends were playing games with all the other young mice, Samuel would wander off exploring, and hope that no one would notice he was missing. He didn't think that anyone really noticed that he was gone.

Sometimes he wondered what it would have been like to have been as brave as Sam. Sam felt lucky just to be able to go exploring, even if it hurt his leg.

And he was quite the explorer. As far as he knew, he'd explored further than any of the other mice. Another mouse might have felt brave, exploring so far from home, but Samuel knew he explored so far to run away from his problems.

Today he had wandered further from home than ever before, and in truth he was very scared.

Something rather large and dark moved in the trees above him. He rather thought it might be a hawk. Like all mice, he was very scared of the hawks. He didn't need his mother's warnings to know how bad it was for a young mouse to be caught out in the open by a hawk. Particularly a young mouse with a bad leg.

There was a rustle in the trees, and for a second the sun disappeared as a dark shadow moved over it. Samuel was almost shaking with fear, and his bad leg was misbehaving quite badly. For some reason it had almost frozen up completely. He was trying to scamper up the river bank to where the longer grass grew, but right now he was trapped half way up the bank. As he scrambled up the bank he was forced to drag his leg, scuffing a furrow of dust as he went. He could feel his heart beating, and not for the first time in his life he cursed his leg.

He looked up. He knew he shouldn't look up, he really should be running for the bushes, but he could feel the fluttering of an eagle's wings, he could feel a sharp beak about to rip into his body and tear him to pieces.

He whimpered as he looked up, and again saw a dark shape circling overhead. He ran towards the top of the bank. But the shape followed him, flitting from tree-to-tree. Samuel caught a glimpse of the shadowy shape, and as it flew through a beam of sunlight, he caught a glimpse of its face, mangled and scared, with one milky eye staring blindly and another good eye watching him. One look at that cruelly scarred face gave him all the energy he needed, and he sprinted as fast as his crippled leg could take him.

He tripped over and almost cried as his leg be-trayed him again. The shadow loomed over him. He could feel it getting closer.

"Hello what have we here?" a voice said out from the grass.

Samuel looked up, and standing at the edge of the long grass was the oldest mouse Samuel had ever seen.

"Run Mister," Samuel shouted, "there's a hawk above."

"Is there now? Is there indeed. Well best we go inside then hadn't we?" The old mouse didn't seem too bothered. He leaned down and grabbed Samuel's hand and helped him up.

"Come on then young fellow, my burrow is just this way," he said pointing to an inviting mouse hole a few dozen feet away, "but mind you don't walk too fast, I'm not as spry as you are."

Samuel gulped. He wasn't meant to talk to strangers, but he rather felt safer with another mouse while there was a bird circling over head.

They walked towards the entrance to the hole, all the time Samuel was looking around for the hawk, but it seemed to have disappeared. The old mouse however still didn't seem concerned, and was strolling along. Despite his age he seemed to manage quite well, although he didn't walk so fast that Samuel couldn't keep up.

"Come on then young fellow, in you go, you look like you could use a nice cup of tea."

Samuel followed the old mouse into his burrow. The tunnel was a lot wider than normal for a mouse burrow and soon it opened out into quite a comfortable living room. The old mouse pointed to a comfortable looking chair. "Take a seat and I'll go make us some afternoon tea."

Samuel sat down. He could hear the old mouse pottering around in his kitchen, talking to himself. Samuel didn't know of any mice living this far away from the burrows. He wondered why this old mouse lived so far away from the company of the other mice. Samuel didn't understand a lot of things that grown up mice did, but he did know that mice liked to be around other mice.

The old mouse appeared with three cups of hot tea.

"There you go young fellow," he said, ruffling the fur on Samuels head. Samuel didn't know why grownups did that either, it was very annoying, but they seemed to think it made them seem friendly.

"Now, tell me, what is your name, and why are you so far from the burrows on a bright sunny day like this?"

"My name is Samuel Sir, and I was just exploring the river bank."

"Samuel eh? I expect they call you Sam then?"

"No Sir. Well, only when they are making fun of me," Samuel said, a little bit down cast. He wished he hadn't mentioned that other mice made fun of him. He looked up to see if the old mouse was making fun of him. He was smiling, but it seemed to be a friendly smile.

"Oh, now, why would they call you Sam when they are making fun of you?" the old mouse asked.

"You know...Sam the bravest mouse ever...the mouse hero...they kinda think its funny that I'm named after a hero and I'm...well, I'm not. I'm just...its, well its my leg, see, everyone knows that..." he trailed off.

"Oh. I see. They think four good paws make you brave? Interesting."

Samuel started as a large shape started to make its way down the burrow, but the old mouse didn't move. Just took another sip of his tea.

"Are you quite done scaring young pups?" the old mouse said over his shoulder to the dark shape.

As the large shape moved into view Samuel saw that it was the bird that had followed him earlier, except it wasn't a bird at all. It was some sort of, well, something like a possum. But smaller. Its face was scarred on one side, and one eye was milky white and obviously blind, but the other eye was clear, and seemed to smile at Samuel.

"Hello Sam," it said.

Samuel didn't know how the beast knew his name, but then the old mouse replied.

"Hello Sugar Glider. Sugar Glider met Samuel. Samuel, meet my good friend Sugar Glider. Don't mind him. He wasn't really trying to scare you, he was just making sure there were no hawks around. He doesn't much like hawks."

Samuel had heard of Sugar Gliders, but never seen one. His mother had described them when she had told him stories of Sam Mouse, and his friend the Sugar Glider.

"Are you Sam Mouse? The one that saved the field mice from the rats and the house mice?" said Samuel.

Sugar Glider laughed. "This should be interest-ing," he said.

Sam smiled. "No. I'm not the mouse hero. Let me tell you about heroes."

Samuel listened as Sam told him a story of a rat and a half rat that had helped the field mice when they were alone and without any friends. And of a field mouse called Michelle who had taken it upon herself to look after orphaned field mice.

"So you see. They were really the hero's. I just happened to bumble upon the whole thing. I'm just a mouse who didn't really know what was going on around me. Real heroes Samuel don't always do one great thing. They do many little good things. Even when those good things are hard, or when others tell you those good things are bad. Heroes are the ones who everyday do the hard things that are right, when other fellows are sitting around doing the easy things that aren't right.

"Courage Samuel isn't about strength of body. Its about the decisions you make and how you handle hard choices. Anyway, enough of my ram-blings...would you like some cake?" asked Sam.

Samuel did like cake, but he would have said yes anyway, because he was a polite mouse.

"I wish I lived in the house Mr Sam," Samuel said. "Don't you wish you could go back?"

Sam sighed. "Sometimes Samuel. Sometimes. But do you know in life, you can never go back. When you do, things are never the same. I miss some of my things. But happiness doesn't come from having more things, it comes from wanting less things. And here, in my burrow, I want for very little."

#

Later that evening, as the sun cast long shadows over the river bank, two old friends sat on the edge of the river watching the water flow past.

"I do miss her Sugar Glider. I didn't really know her for very long. But I miss her."

Sugar Glider, being a good friend, knew that there was nothing he needed to say.

"Oh. I finished my book this morning Sugar Glider," said Sam. Sugar Glider sat upright, and clapped his front paws together.

"That's very exciting Sam. I can't wait to read about your grandfather," said Sugar Glider.

"Oh. Its actually not really about my Grandfather. I think I'll still write that book. No, this book is about the field mice, and the rats and sugar gliders that helped them escape. And about the cost that those animals paid for their bravery."

Sam looked at his friend's scarred face, and his blind eye.

"I don't have many regrets Sugar Glider," Sam said. "But one of them is that you lost your eye. I wish I could change that. I really do."

"Nonsense," Sugar Glider snorted. "I do miss my eye, and if I had a choice, I should very much like it back. But after I rolled around on the ground with that hawk, he was so startled that he flew off with me still holding him. Higher and higher he went, trying to shake me off. When I finally let go, I was so high that the trees looked like grass."

Sam's stomach felt funny thinking about being that far off the ground. He had heard this story many times before, but Sugar Glider was always so excited when he told it, that it made Sam happy to hear his friend tell it.

"To think Sam," Sugar Glider continued, "no Sugar Glider has even been that high. Higher than the highest tree. I glided for so long, and so far. I even managed to catch an up-draft and gain some altitude. I didn't even feel the pain in my eye until long after I hit the ground. I wish I'd never lost my eye Sam, but I would never trade that experience. To glide for so long, and so high...oh how marvelous."

"You know Sugar Glider. I have quite a large store of seeds and nuts set aside this year, now that winter is over, perhaps if you help me gather some more, we might give them to one the cockatoos to take you for a flight on its back. Get you back up high again."

Sugar Glider smiled absently as he thought about soaring far above the ground.

" Sam," said Sugar Glider, "I was wrong all that time ago. Its not all about lift and drag. Actually flying is really all about the angle of attack. Here, let me explain..."

As the sugar glider rambled on about the importance of the angle of attack, Sam sighed, and nodded. Well, he wasn't sure what life was about, but he did know that good and true friends were few and far between.

The End

Epilogue

On a small rise overlooking a broad meadow covered with long soft grass and daises stood a rat. Except he wasn't really a rat. He had a small back pack on, and in one paw he held a long pole that he used as a walking stick. In the distance he saw a small stream, running towards a beautiful blue lake nestled into distant snow capped mountains. The mouse, except he wasn't really a mouse, settled down under a copse of beech trees growing on the crest of the rise. From his back pack he took out a small wax paper bundle tied with string. Inside were some nuts and berries.

He had gathered the nuts and berries during his wanderings over the last few days. They were plentiful this time of year, but soon he would stop for a few days and dry some berries and make flour out of crushed nuts so that he didn't need to rely on finding food as he walked. He had many miles to go before he reached the mountains in the distance. And even one mile is a long way for a rat. Or a mouse.

Perhaps he would make a camp by the lake, in readiness for winter. Or maybe he would push on to the mountains before the weather got too bad.

He unwrapped the wax paper bundle, taking out a piece of hard aged cheddar and cut a small piece off, carefully wrapping the remainder and tying the bundle up neatly. He nibbled on the cheese, enjoying its sharp bite. He didn't know when he would find cheese again, if ever. But the thought only made the cheese taste even better. He closed his eyes, and enjoyed every mouthful.

When he'd finished his small meal, he tidied up after himself, not wanting to spoil the beauty of the woods for any that followed in his footsteps. He hefted his back pack onto his back. Its weight settling comfortably on his shoulders. He paused, admiring the scenery for a moment.

"Come on Roland," he said to himself. "Let's see what adventures are waiting in those mountains."

Author's Notes

I hope you enjoyed the story of Sam Mouse. I certainly enjoyed writing it. This is my first novel, and it wasn't easy, but I have learned a lot in the process of writing.

Before you read on, can I ask that you leave a review? Independent authors rely on readers leaving reviews to help them sell their books and for feedback on what their readers think. I would love you to leave an honest review of Sam Mouse. If you do leave a review (good or bad!), send me an email with a link to it, and I'll send you a copy of a short story set in Sam's world. You can review Sam Mouse at http://www.craigturner.id.au/reviewsam.

I first started writing this story about ten years ago. I can't say what exactly inspired the story. Nor did I even know what the story was about when I started writing it. All I had in my head was an image of a mouse receiving a letter tasking him to deal with a nasty vicious cat. I knew that this mouse led a very comfortable soft life, what I didn't realize was that and that his comfortable life was stopping him from becoming all that he could be.

Stephen King, in his book about the art and craft of writing, titled 'On Writing' says that stories are found objects. That stories are like fossils, and that the job of the writer is to chip away at the stone.

Michelangelo is said to have replied to the question on how he sculpted the statue David, was that all he did was remove the pieces of marble that weren't David.

I think there is some truth in this view of the creative process. But removing dirt and stone is hard work. Sam's story was only ever meant to be a short story. Like a lot of aspiring authors, I pottered around the edges of this story. Chipping away a bit of dirt here, removing some soft sand there. But then I'd hit a piece of granite. And granite is hard. So I'd forget about Sam for a while. I would not write a word for a year or two. I'd start something else. But as I started excavating a new dig, I'd glace over at the mess that was my dig for Sam's story. I could almost hear a muffled mouse underneath the rubble saying 'Finish me.'

I really wanted to write science fiction. You know, that trashy stuff. I really like trashy science fiction. I consumed science fiction from the golden age of SciFi as a kid (and as an adult), Asimov, Bradbury, Heinlein, Andre Norton and so on. I ached to write those stories. Now its Peter Hamilton, Richard Morgan, Andy Weir, Kim Stanley-Robinson etc. That's the kind of science fiction I felt I wanted to write.

But I needed to keep digging away at Sam, because I couldn't leave him half done.

As I write this, I am sitting in a shed with a beautiful view of an old bluestone church. One day this shed will be a proper studio, but right now, its a shed with a concrete floor. In winter its freezing cold, and I write hunched over a keyboard with a beanie on and my breathe making little clouds in front of the computer. In summer the shed is blazing hot.

There is an irony that this little shed with the beautiful view has mice in it. When I started cleaning the shed out, I found their droppings. But since I have completed Sam Mouse, I haven't seen any droppings for a while. I hope they are decent mice. Perhaps, now that I have exorcised the ghosts of Sam's story, they have moved on. Perhaps, they have taken to the fields that surround our house, and are living a simpler and happier life than they would be if they kept trying to invade my study.

I'm planning to write science fiction for a bit. Which I plan to write under another name, but I will publish it through Paxel Publishing. (http://www.paxel.com.au). This is so that I don't confuse readers as to what they are getting when they read my books. The name I plan on using is Gordon Andrews.

Sam Mouse was always going to be a stand alone story. But something funny happened during the diggings. I found a small fossil of a story attached to this one. In fact, I found a couple. I'm scared to dig any further. You know what it's like, when you start a small job and realize it's going to be a big one.

You see, I think there is story to be told about young Samuel. It's a blessing and a curse to be a field mouse with a bad leg and a sense of adventure...also, I do think Sugar Glider has a story to tell. Maybe not a novel, but certainly I'm curious to know how he goes with his flying.

And most importantly for me, what of Roland? Half mouse, half rat? What is he looking for, and what will he find?

If you would like to find out when my next story is released, please sign up to my email list. You can subscribe to my mailing list at this URL:

http://www.craigturner.id.au/subscribe

You won't get spammed, nor will I sell your address to Russian hackers. Well....unless my book doesn't sell...What you will get is advanced notice of my next book, copies of short stories not released elsewhere, and maybe some giveaways. If you did find like this story, please check out my website, http://www.craigturner.id.au for more stories and information.

Finally, if you want to drop me an email with any questions or thoughts, or if you'd just like to tell me what you did, or didn't like about the book, please feel free to send me an email at craig@craigturner.id.au

About the Author

After receiving a Bachelors in Social Science, Craig found himself perfectly qualified for managing a pub in inner city Melbourne, (purely in order to gather characters for a novel)

After having a gun pulled on him while dealing with an unruly drunk, he decided to join the Army, where the pay was better, (and, to his surprise, so was the food). He also maintains that he joined the army to get better inspirations for stories.

Which might explain why his first book is about a mouse called Sam. Of course, it took him a few years to realize that he needed to stop gathering information and start writing before he would actually be able to publish a book.
Craig has always had a passion for writing, but university and army training beat down his creativity until it hid deep inside. That passion finally resurfaced in the form of several award winning short stories, and now a debut novel (Sam Mouse).

Craig lives in Central Victoria in Australia, and blogs at https://www.craigturner.id.au

You can follow Craig on FaceBook at https://www.facebook.com/craigturnerauthor and on twitter @CraigTurner6